"Lunchtime," Whitney announced, and grabbed a luscious peach from her picnic basket.

A glint of mischief in her eyes, she bit into the peach and sighed, her eyes never leaving Stone's. A strange sound came from low in his throat, and she glanced over at him. Her eyes widened when she saw his expression. He was staring at her mouth as though he were starving and she had the last bite of food. Her tongue automatically darted out to catch the juice on her bottom lip, and he made that sound again.

Before she could react, Stone swiftly framed her face with his hands. Then he licked the remaining drops of peach juice from her lips.

"Delicious," he murmured. "You taste like everything delicious in this world." He feasted on her mouth, gently savoring her. He caressed and nibbled her bottom lip, and she sighed again. The half-eaten peach fell from her hands onto the grass as a different hunger replaced the desire for food.

Stone pulled her into his lap and held her close. "I think I could become addicted to picnics if they always taste this good. . . ."

WHAT ARE *LOVESWEPT* ROMANCES?

They are stories of true romance and touching emotion. We believe those two very important ingredients are constants in our highly sensual and very believable stories in the *LOVESWEPT* line. Our goal is to give you, the reader, stories of consistently high quality that may sometimes make you laugh, sometimes make you cry, but are always fresh and creative and contain many delightful surprises within their pages.

Most romance fans read an enormous number of books. Those they truly love, they keep. Others may be traded with friends and soon forgotten. We hope that each *LOVESWEPT* romance will be a treasure—a "keeper." We will always try to publish

LOVE STORIES YOU'LL NEVER FORGET
BY AUTHORS YOU'LL ALWAYS REMEMBER

The Editors

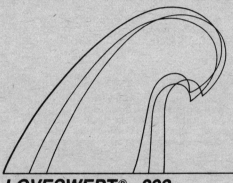

LOVESWEPT® • 292

Patt Bucheister
Time Out

 BANTAM BOOKS
TORONTO • NEW YORK • LONDON • SYDNEY • AUCKLAND

TIME OUT

A Bantam Book / November 1988

*LOVESWEPT® and the wave device are registered
trademarks of Bantam Books, a division of
Bantam Doubleday Dell Publishing Group, Inc.
Registered in U.S. Patent
and Trademark Office and elsewhere.*

ISBN 0-553-21944-8

Published simultaneously in the United States and Canada

*Bantam Books are published by Bantam Books, a division
of Bantam Doubleday Dell Publishing Group, Inc. Its trademark, consisting of the words "Bantam Books" and the
portrayal of a rooster, is Registered in U.S. Patent and
Trademark Office and in other countries. Marca Registrada.
Bantam Books, 666 Fifth Avenue, New York, New York 10103.*

PRINTED IN THE UNITED STATES OF AMERICA

O   0 9 8 7 6 5 4 3 2 1

To my sons, Scott and Todd,
who had to put up with a mother
who had a paintbrush in one hand
and a pen in the other.
This one is for you.

One

Her father had warned her she was heading for a fall, but Whitney Grant didn't think this was quite what he meant. From her present position of being flat on her back, she stared up into the black button eyes of the teddy bear whose nose was pressed to hers. As a resident of San Francisco, she was accustomed to the threat of earthquakes hanging over the city, but this was the first time she'd ever experienced an avalanche.

Everything had been going along just fine until she had reached up to arrange the top bear on the "teddy tree." Then the whole thing had come crashing down on top of her. All of a sudden she was sprawled on the floor of her friend's children's store under twenty teddy bears in a tangled web of stuffed arms, legs, and about twenty feet of electrical wire.

Frowning up at the bear perched on her face, she wondered how she was going to get out from under this furry mountain. The bears were dressed in various outfits that could be damaged if she started flinging them off her. Her friend Nancy wouldn't be too happy if the bears' clothing had to be repaired. Further, Whitney didn't want to dislodge any of the wires that made the bears' arms move. The intricate wiring had taken hours to hook up and she would just as soon not have to do it all over again.

Nancy had said she was going to be in the back room putting away the stock that had arrived earlier, so she wouldn't be much help at the moment. The bell hanging above the door would ring if anyone came into the store, but that didn't help Whitney since it wasn't ringing. So . . .

"Help!" she shouted.

When she didn't get any response, she called again. "Nancy, come get these darn bears off me."

While she was yelling, she thought she heard a tinkling sound, but she wasn't sure whether it had been the bell above the door or her imagination. Just in case it had been the door, she said peevishly, "I sure could use some help down here."

She didn't hear any footsteps or offers of assistance. She couldn't stay there all day staring at the darn fuzzy bear. Moving her arms and legs tentatively to see if she could get up by herself without damaging anything, she discovered her right leg was caught by some wire wrapped around it. Glaring up at the bear as though it were all its fault, she muttered a rather colorful swear word.

"Naughty, naughty. Teddy bears shouldn't swear."

Whitney froze. Unless Nancy had caught a really serious cold in the last half hour, that deep voice belonged to a man. She had no idea who it was, but it didn't really matter as long as he helped her get out from under the pile of bears.

"I'll stop swearing if you get me out of here," she said sweetly.

"Do you belong to the toe of the scruffy-looking sneaker I can see sticking out?" the man asked.

"My sneakers are not scruffy," Whitney said, as indignantly as was possible under her present circumstances. "They're well worn."

"Excuse me." The reply was edged in humor. "I guess I don't know antiques all that well."

It was a shame, she thought, he couldn't see the glowering look on her face. The bear remained completely oblivious. "Look, Bud," she snapped. "Are you going to get me out of this mess or not?"

Stone Hamilton found himself smiling down at the pile of bears. "I'll give it a try."

"Don't pull the wires if you can help it," she instructed quickly. "They're attached to the bears. Oh, and try not to damage the bears. Nancy will have your head if their clothes are mussed up after she spent so many hours making them."

Stone had been about to toss a bear over his shoulder. After her warning, he carefully set it to one side instead. He hadn't the faintest idea who Nancy was, but he was rather fond of his head and would just as soon keep it a little while longer. When he picked up the next bear, he saw what the unseen woman had meant about the wire. There were small strands of electrical wiring wrapped around some of the furry arms and legs and coming out of their backs. He couldn't lift them off her until he had freed each bear.

Whitney couldn't hear any sounds of activity around her. "This is not the time to play with each and every bear," she said. "You can buy the bear you came for after you get me out of here."

There was no response.

She tried again. "Hello? Are you still there?"

"I'm still here."

"Could you get on with it? I'm going cross-eyed staring at this bear who landed on my face."

"He doesn't seem to be interfering with your mouth," the man drawled.

Chivalry was definitely on the decline, she thought. With as much dignity as she could muster, she corrected him. "It's a she."

He finally got a stubborn wire from around a bear's neck and set it aside with the others. "Shut your eyes then if you don't want to look at the lady bear. I'm working as fast as I can. The bears are all tangled up in the wire."

Whitney hoped he wasn't ruining hours of work. "I don't want to sound ungrateful, but could you please be careful not to break any of the wiring loose from the bears, especially the one in the navy uniform. It took me four hours to get him to salute properly."

Saluting teddy bears? What had he walked into? Stone wondered as he continued to untangle wire from a bear's leg. "When I come across the sailor, I'll be gentle with him," he said dryly.

As he removed one teddy bear after another, he gradually revealed more of the woman on the floor. An odd curiosity drove him to uncover her, even though he really shouldn't be wasting the time. He had allotted thirty minutes to introduce himself to the member of the wedding party he was supposed to escort to the rehearsal. Sylvia, the bride, had told him to meet the woman here. He had used up at least five minutes shifting and untangling the stuffed menagerie at his feet. Still, as much as he disliked deviating from his schedule, he had to see the woman under the teddy bears. The other woman would just have to wait.

He had already uncovered two denim-clad legs above the ancient sneakers, with wire wrapped around one ankle. Slender hips and a trim waist appeared next. When he saw a white shirt and red suspenders attached to the waistband of the jeans, he began to wonder if she was a she after all. Maybe he was digging out a young boy whose voice hadn't changed. The removal of another bear revealed the gentle swell of breasts beneath the tight knit shirt and red suspenders. This was definitely not a boy.

There were still six bears covering her arms and upper body when Whitney became impatient and tried to get up. She didn't realize one of her rescuer's polished shoes stood on the wire wrapped around her ankle, and when she jerked her leg, she ended up tripping him.

Stone held out his arms to break his fall, aware he was going to land directly on the woman. The palms of his hands hit the floor on either side of her shoulders seconds before he heard a soft whoosh of air escape from her as his body dropped onto hers.

Several bears were squashed between them, but his hips were pressed intimately against hers without anything but their clothing separating them. An unmistakable male reaction tightened his body.

Stone rested his weight on one arm so he could tug a bear out from under his chest. At the same time, Whitney pulled away the bear covering her face.

The moment her eyes met his, she felt a peculiar sense of recognition, even though she was sure she had never met him before. His blond hair was mussed, which was understandable under the circumstances, and his eyes were the deep green color of the ocean during a storm. She could see from her position underneath him, that he was wearing a white shirt, a maroon silk tie, and a gray suit. A tangy scent of after-shave drifted around her and sent unexpected shivers of awareness along her veins.

She smiled faintly. "Hi."

Something flickered in his eyes, then was gone. "Hi," he replied huskily.

It wasn't only his weight that was making it difficult for Whitney to catch her breath. She was experiencing some rather odd sensations as she watched his gaze lower to her mouth. Maybe she wasn't the most experienced woman in town when it came to men, but she recognized the look of a man who wanted to kiss her. Her imagination began working overtime, wondering how his lips would feel on hers. If it was anything like the way his body felt, she was in big trouble.

In an attempt to lighten the situation, she asked politely, "Do you come here often?" Her voice sounded oddly breathless.

His lips twitched in a crooked smile. "No, this is the first time."

His mouth was only inches away from hers and his breath lightly brushed her skin when he spoke. Heat rushed through her body. "It's a nice place to buy things for kids," she said in an effort to make conversation.

"So I've heard."

"Are we going to stay like this all day?"

Stone admitted to himself that it sounded like a darn good idea. He was amazed that he was in no hurry to get off her, even though sprawling on top of a woman in public wasn't his usual style. His gaze shifted to her mouth again. Nor was wanting to kiss a complete stranger. Unfortunately he didn't have all day. He was on a tight schedule and had already wasted fifteen minutes. Wasted? No, he corrected himself. The time had not been wasted. Frustrating, maybe. Different, certainly. Intriguing, definitely.

It was no use. He couldn't resist the temptation to feel her mouth under his. Keeping the weight of his upper body off her as much as he could, he lowered his head and took her mouth. The impact of falling to the floor was nothing compared to the jolt of desire that coursed through him like a lightning bolt. The persuasive pressure of his mouth enticed her lips to part. He tasted the velvet intimacy of her mouth, and the sparks that had been kindled when he first felt her soft feminine body under his burst into flames.

Realizing how close he was to losing control, Stone stopped abruptly and freed her mouth. As close as they were, she had to be aware of how his body was reacting, unless she had gone numb from the waist down. He certainly hadn't.

Slowly she opened her eyes and met his gaze. She looked as dazed as he felt.

He pushed his long body off her with marked reluctance. Standing, he reached down to help her up. When she lifted her arm, the motion pulled one of the suspenders tight over her breast. He gripped her small hand fiercely as he fought the desire to slide his hand under that suspender. Deciding it wasn't a good idea to touch her at all, he dropped her hand abruptly once she was on her feet.

Now that she was standing in front of him, he saw she was a little bit of a thing. The top of her head barely came to his shoulders. Her dark brown hair was short and framed her face with loose bouncy curls. When she looked up at him, he was momentarily captivated by the liveliness emanating from her lovely blue eyes.

After a quick glance at his watch, he was just going to ask her about the person he was supposed to meet there when a tall, plump woman came out of a back room. Dressed in a pink gingham smock that covered the top half of a pink dress, she looked like a fluffy chunk of cotton candy. She headed toward them, then stopped abruptly when she caught a glimpse of part of her inventory scattered on the floor.

"What happened?" she asked in a resigned tone.

"I got a little heavy-handed with the last bear," Whitney said. "Don't worry, Nancy. It won't take long to build it up again. I told you Melvin was the one who should set this up. He's taller than I am."

Nancy shook her head. "I wanted you to do the display. Melvin makes me nervous."

"Why would Melvin make you nervous? He's about as aggressive as a bowl of oatmeal."

"Anyone who has three college degrees and can make figures walk, talk, and dance intimidates me."

Whitney grinned. "I have three degrees and make figures walk, talk, and dance. You don't seem to be intimidated by me."

Nancy gestured with one hand, casually dismissing Whitney's extensive education. "You don't act like you do. Melvin does. He talks in ten-letter words."

Whitney turned her attention back to her rescuer. She wanted to thank him for helping her, but when she saw his strange expression, she wondered why he looked as though he had just been hit in the face with a wet flounder.

"What's wrong?" she asked him bluntly. "You look odd."

As he stared blankly at her, Stone decided his reputation as a sharp businessman was highly overrated. "I feel odd," he said abstractedly.

For a moment, Whitney absorbed the sound of his voice. It reminded her of dark velvet sliding over smooth hot satin. Then she mentally shook herself away from her tantalizing thoughts and thanked him for helping her get out from under the bears. His response was only a slight nod in acknowledgement, and she turned away to gather up the bears.

Thinking he was a customer, Nancy asked him if he needed help finding anything. He shook his head, his gaze remaining on Whitney. Giving him the opportunity to browse, Nancy began to help pick up the bears.

Stone watched as Whitney began to set the bears back onto the platform in a particular order, arranging the wires around them again. He knew he should be asking about the other woman he had come to meet, but it was a little disconcerting for him to realize he was preoccupied with the view of this woman from the back. He enjoyed it almost as much as he had delighted in the view from the front. Almost.

Nancy handed Whitney another bear. "This display is going to be even better than you described, Whitney. I love the idea of having the teddy bears in military uniforms salute. It fits in perfectly with my Fourth of July sale."

Behind her, Whitney heard a strange choking sound and jerked her head around.

Her rescuer was looking at her strangely. "*You're* Whitney Grant?"

She straightened up. "Yes, I am," she replied cautiously.

"You're not what I expected."

"Really? How odd. Exactly what did you expect?"

"A maid of honor." Realizing that statement didn't make any more sense than anything else that had happened since he had walked into the store, he attempted to explain. "I'm Stone Hamilton. I'm going to be David Crandall's best man on Saturday." He took a step toward her and his shoe hit something. He automatically picked up the stray bear as he added, "Sylvia said you would be expecting me."

Whitney had forgotten all about the phone call last night from Sylvia. Her friend had insisted that she be escorted to the wedding rehearsal and the dinner afterwards by the best man, Stone Hamilton. Sylvia had informed Whitney to expect Stone at the warehouse around eleven in the morning. Whitney wasn't going to be at the warehouse at that time, so Sylvia said she would tell Stone to meet her at the children's store instead. Then they could make arrangements for the rehearsal at the church.

Whitney took the bear from him. "Sylvia did mention you would be coming by. I'm glad you did. I'd probably still be under the pile of bears if you hadn't."

After setting the bear in its place on the display, she turned back to him and caught him stealing a peek at his watch. She shoved her hands into the front pockets of her jeans. "Are you late for something?"

"Well," he began, momentarily sidetracked by the sight of those red suspenders pulling against her tempting breasts, "I should be leaving. I have an appointment at one o'clock."

"What time is it now?"

His gaze went to her bare wrists. She wasn't wearing a watch. "Five minutes to twelve."

"How far is your office from here?"

He named the building his office was in and she knew it was only a couple of blocks away. "Would you like to have a bite to eat with me?" she asked abruptly. "I'm starving. The service at the restaurant across the street is pretty good and we can discuss the arrangements for tomorrow night while we eat. You've got plenty of time before your appointment."

He frowned as he looked at his watch again. He had planned to return to his office at twelve to do some work before his appointment. He was about to say he didn't have the time, when Whitney scolded kindly, "Lighten up, Hamilton. The world won't come to an end if you change your schedule." She turned to Nancy. "We're going out to lunch. When I come back, I'll finish the display."

Nancy gave a martyred sigh. "Try to get back sometime today, Whitney. The sale starts tomorrow. I know how you are about time."

"Don't fret. I'll be back after lunch."

Before Stone could point out he would rather make the arrangements now so he could get back to his office, Whitney was headed toward the front door, grabbing a red leather jacket off a counter on her way. Even in July, San Francisco weather could be cool and this was one of those days.

Whitney pushed open the door as she shrugged into the jacket. When she was outside, she looked back and realized Stone wasn't with her. For a man who was in such a hurry, he didn't move very fast, she thought irritably. She could see him through the glass door and caught his moment of hesitation before he started after her. He didn't seem terribly eager to have lunch with her, but that was too darn bad. She was hungry and they could discuss when he would pick her up while she ate. That way they wouldn't waste the time he considered so important. He wasn't the only one who had other things to do today.

When he finally pushed open the door, she noticed he looked at his watch again. Either he was admiring a new watch or he definitely had a thing about time.

She tried to reassure him he wouldn't be late when he finally walked up to her. "The restaurant is just across the street and you don't have to wait long to be served."

She took his arm to ensure he would keep up with her and headed across the street, dodging around the cars that had stopped for the traffic light. Stone had to turn sideways to squeeze between the cars. He felt like he was being swept along a strong current, unable to control his destination. He knew he could have insisted he had to return to his office, but this curiosity about Whitney Grant was stronger than his desire to keep to his schedule.

Whitney stepped up onto the sidewalk and walked toward the door of a pizza parlor. "Pepé Shapiro makes the best pizzas on the west coast. Don't order pizza with peppers on it though. I don't know where he gets them, but they'll melt the lining of your stomach."

Stone held the door open for her, amused and fascinated by her snippets of information. She didn't waste any time on polite chitchat, jumping right in instead with whatever came to her mind. As she preceded him into the pizza parlor, his gaze roamed over her and he found himself comparing her to the woman he had escorted to a concert the previous night. Angela Vandermeer had been elegantly dressed and socially correct. Thinking back, he couldn't recall a single memorable thing she had said. In contrast to Whitney Grant, Angela seemed as dull as dishwater.

Delicious aromas assaulted him as he stepped into the restaurant. Yeast, tomato sauce, garlic, cheese, and other scents he couldn't name made his mouth water. He couldn't remember the last time he had eaten a pizza.

Whitey saw Pepé, an apron over his protruding stomach and a jaunty chef's hat perched on his bald head. He was behind the counter and she lifted her hand in greeting. "The usual, please, Pepé. No peppers or anchovies and lots of cheese."

"You got it," replied the jovial man.

There was a vacant booth toward the back and Whitney headed for it. After a brief hesitation, Stone slid onto the hard wood seat across from her, ducking so he didn't bump his head on a drooping fern hanging over the table. Out of habit, he glanced at his watch and allowed himself thirty minutes to have lunch.

Whitney rested her elbow on the table and her chin on her hand as she gazed curiously at him. "Is it your birthday?"

Stone blinked and then stared. "No, why?"

"I was wondering if you just got that watch for your birthday. You keep looking at it as though it's your most prized possession."

He smiled slightly. "In a way, it is. I work under a tight schedule."

"Why?"

He gave her an impatient look. She asked the damnedest questions at the damnedest times. "It's the most efficient way to get work done. If each day is planned, there is less chance of wasting valuable hours and a better chance of accomplishing more than if you just drift through a day."

Whitney found his attitude toward time fascinating but foreign to her own outlook. She decided to delve a little deeper. "What about time for fun? Do you include that in your schedule?"

He frowned. "I set aside time for recreation occasionally." His frown deepened as he realized how stuffy that sounded. Meeting her dancing blue eyes, he saw that she thought so too.

With more perception than he had expected, she asked, "How much time have you just set aside for lunch?"

"Thirty minutes."

Her smile broadened.

"Are you laughing at me?" he asked, feeling defensive.

Shaking her head, Whitney dropped her arm and leaned back. "I was trying to visualize working on a timetable. Each of my days is so different. Sometimes Melvin and I work all night to meet a deadline or to set up a display, and then we crash for about ten hours."

"Who's Melvin?"

Pepé chose that moment to deliver a piping hot pizza to their table. The round steaming pan was set on a small pedestal before he placed plates and silverware in front of them. He grinned broadly at Whitney. "I'll bring your usual drink, but what would your young man like? Perhaps a beer or some wine, or will he have what you're having?"

Whitney matched his smile with one of her own. "I think you'd better ask him, Pepé. I imagine he's been ordering for himself for several years now."

Pepé looked expectantly at Stone.

Stone was about to order a glass of iced tea when he happened to catch the mocking glint in Whitney's eyes. Perversely he ordered beer. Pepé nodded and left, then returned almost immediately with a foaming mug of beer and a large glass of milk.

Stone looked at the glass of milk Pepé had placed by Whitney's plate, then raised his eyes to meet her gaze. "How old are you?"

Helping herself to a generous slice of pizza, she replied casually. "Twenty-six. I like milk. How old are you?"

"Thirty-two."

She plopped the cheese-smothered pizza slice on her plate and began to eat without commenting.

Stone returned to his earlier question. "Who's Melvin?"

Her reply was slightly garbled since she had just taken a bite of pizza. "My partner."

That answer didn't help him one bit. "I thought the woman who helped you pick up the bears was named Nancy."

"I don't work in that store. I was there to set up a display. That's what I do."

"You set up displays of teddy bears?" he asked in bewilderment.

"Among other things." She glanced at his empty plate. "If you're going to stick to your schedule, you'd better dig in or you'll run out of time."

Stone took a slice of pizza more to get her off the subject of food than because he was hungry. "What other things do you do?"

She had polished off the first slice and reached for another. "Melvin and I design, construct, and set up displays of mechanical figures." When she saw his blank expression, she asked, "Did you notice the nativity scene in the lobby of your office building last Christmas?" He nodded. "Did you notice that Mary looked down at the baby in the manger and then up at Joseph, that the lambs' tails twitched and their heads went back and forth?" He nodded again. "Those figures were designed by Grant and Gunn Animations. That's me and Melvin. I'm Grant. He's Gunn."

"I'll be damned," he muttered softly, staring at her.

Whitney returned her attention to her pizza. She was accustomed to people finding her choice of occupation a little on the strange side. Her appearance deceived those who thought such a small woman must have an equally tiny brain and would be incapable of handling anything heavier than a nail file. Long ago she had come to terms with herself. It was other people who had to adjust, not she.

She was reaching for a third slice of pizza when she saw Stone push back the sleeve of his coat and glance again at his watch. The man had an absolute fetish about time. She wondered why.

"Am I boring you?" she asked quietly.

Startled, he looked up at her. She was about as boring as a three-ring circus. "No. Why?"

She nodded at his watch. "You're checking the time again. Perhaps we had better make the arrangements for tomorrow night before the minute hand tells you it's time to leave."

His jaw clenched. He wasn't used to anyone making fun of his punctuality.

"I'm not the only one who has things to do today," he said. "You have to get back to the children's store to finish your display. Or don't you plan to return to the store?"

"I have all afternoon."

His eyes narrowed as he studied her intently. "You have your own business so you have to have some concept of time and organization in order to get anything done. You can't tell customers you'll see them someday and appear whenever you feel like it."

"One advantage of running our own business is we set our own hours. We don't let a clock tell us what to do or when."

"That's not very good business management."

"Probably not, but it works. We promise to deliver a design or a display on a given day and we do. We may not pay much attention to a clock, but we do look at a calender now and then."

Stone stared at her. Her attitude was the exact opposite of his own. Ever since he had left home for college, he had been driven to create an orderly world for himself, a world completely different from the one he had been raised in. He'd had enough of having the electricity shut off, furniture repossessed, and pets brought home and then forgotten by his mother.

The similarity between Whitney's attitude and his mother's had him reaching into the breast pocket of his suit jacket for his small leather appointment book. He opened it to tomorrow's date. "The rehearsal is at seven. I'll pick you up at six-thirty." He made a notation with his gold pen. "Where do you live?"

She gave him the address and watched as he wrote it down under her name. "In case you get held up and will be late or can't make it," she said, "I'll give you a phone number where I can be reached." He jotted down the number of the warehouse beneath the address she had given him.

He flipped his notebook closed and tucked it back into his coat pocket. "I'll be there."

"At six-thirty on the dot, right?"

Wondering if she was making fun of him again, he said with a hint of temper, "I'll be on time. Make sure you are."

Now she'd made him mad, she thought. In an effort to lighten the atmosphere between them, she said, "You have nice handwriting."

Stone's irritation faded away and he smiled. "Thanks."

"My handwriting is terrible. My printing isn't too bad, but I'm usually in too much of a hurry to bother with neatness. The only consolation I have is that Melvin's scribbles are worse. We've had to come up with a kind of shorthand we can both decipher when we plan a design, or we would spend all our time asking each other what we'd written down."

He gave up any pretense of eating and sat back against the hard wooden booth. It wasn't only what she said that held his attention, but the way she said it. Blue lights danced in her eyes when she looked at him, and he found it impossible to turn away. His gaze dropped to her mouth. He remembered how natural it had felt to kiss her and wanted more than anything to feel her mouth under his again. He had never met anyone like her, and sincerely doubted there was anyone else like her in the world.

Whitney mentally squirmed under his intent gaze. She wished she knew what he was thinking, but decided it was just as well she didn't. Thank heavens he couldn't tell *her* thoughts were dwelling on the magical kiss they had shared earlier. She could still feel the imprint of his long body against hers and a rush of warmth flowed over her, heating her blood and her skin.

When he chuckled, she blinked as if coming out of a trance and focused on his face. "Did I miss something funny?"

"I have a feeling you were thinking the same thing I was. You blush beautifully."

She didn't attempt to dissemble. "It was quite a kiss."

This time Stone laughed outright and Whitney's eyes widened at the difference laughter made in him. His handsome face grew even more attractive with the glow of humor. His laugh was a sound of such pure enjoyment that feathers of awareness brushed along her skin.

"You should do that more often," she said.

"Do what?"

"Laugh. I have the feeling you don't laugh enough."

He shook his head in mock exasperation. "Do you always say what you're thinking?"

"Usually."

"It takes a little getting used to, but I like it."

Grinning broadly, she wiped her hands on a napkin. "Plain speaking must be good for you. You haven't looked at your watch in the last five minutes."

For a smile like hers, he could be tempted to throw his watch under the nearest bus. "You seem to be good for me, Whitney. I rarely forget about time."

"Why is that?" she asked curiously.

"I'm an efficiency expert. I show people how to make the best use of their time."

The only thing she could think to say was the same response he had made when she told him what she did for a living. "I'll be damned."

A corner of his mouth curved up. "I know how you feel. We seem to have similar reactions to each other's occupations."

Pepé came over to their table to find out if they needed anything more.

They shook their heads and Stone asked for the bill. Returning his attention to Whitney, he said, "As much as I would like to stay and talk to you, I really do have to get back to work. It wouldn't do to have an efficiency expert late for an appointment."

Whitney protested when she saw him take out his wallet. "You don't have to buy my lunch. This was my idea."

"And it was a good one," he said as he withdrew several bills from his wallet. He laid them on the table and stood up. "But I'll pay for the meal."

Whitney recognized a brick wall when she saw one and didn't make an issue of paying for her half of lunch. She slid out of the booth and stood in front of him. "Thanks for the rescue and the pizza."

"You're welcome," he said softly. He lifted his hand to rub the back of his forefinger along her cheek. "I'll see you tomorrow night."

She nodded, for once speechless. She hadn't expected him to touch her. Or that she would like it so much. Turning away before she did something incredibly foolish like throwing herself into his arms, she left the restaurant.

She hadn't been looking forward to being Sylvia's maid of honor, but now she decided there might be some interesting fringe benefits after all.

Two

At exactly six-thirty the following evening, Stone knocked at a large metal door. He had checked the number above the door twice and it kept reading the same way. This was the address Whitney had given him. The location was a block off the Embarcadero, the building one of a long line of warehouses. Converting abandoned warehouses into living quarters was becoming popular with young professionals and business people, but after meeting Whitney, Stone thought she would choose a warehouse just because it was different.

He had parked next to a dark red van with the word GRANT AND GUNN ANIMATIONS superimposed over a stick figure bending over a computer. He wondered if this was her business address rather than her home.

He pounded harder on the door and finally got a response. Instead of Whitney, though, a tall, thin man flung open the door and glowered at Stone through the thick lenses of his glasses. "Whatta ya want?"

Stone stared at the belligerent man. He looked like a

harassed bookkeeper straight out of a Dickens novel. His short sandy-colored hair stuck out around his head as though a comb had never made an acquaintance with it. His clothing was rumpled and hung loosely on his rangy frame. The bespectacled man could have been anywhere from his midtwenties to his midthirties, but Stone was more curious about who he was rather than how old he was.

Making an educated guess, he decided this guy must be Whitney's partner, Melvin Gunn. Hopefully he was better at creating their mechanical objects than greeting people. His public relations left a lot to be desired.

"I'm looking for Whitney Grant."

The other man jerked his head toward the interior of the building. "She's here." The door was shoved open farther, the hinges protesting loudly.

Stone took that to be an invitation to come in, although the man didn't seem to care one way or the other.

Stone had to wait a moment for his eyes to adjust to the bright lights inside. Dust motes floated in the air, highlighted by the long strands of fluorescent lights strung overhead. His attention was captured by an astonishing clutter of figures strewn among the elongated workbenches running down the sides of the enormous room and on the few tables situated in rows in the middle.

The tall man who let him in was striding across the concrete floor toward a large flatbed platform at the far end of the warehouse. A number of mechanical figures were arranged on its bare surface. Looking closer, Stone saw a papier-mâché lobster, a couple of clamshells, and an imposing figure of King Neptune sitting on a throne. The whole setup resembled a basic design for a float for a parade.

"Whitney," Melvin called. "Your date is here."

There was a muffled reply from the vicinity of the platform. "Oh, cripes! What time is it, Melvin?"

Melvin sat down at a drawing board, bent over to peer at the papers spread out in front of him, and replied absently, "I don't know."

Moving closer to the platform, Stone spotted a familiar pair of grungy sneakers sticking out on one side. "Whitney?"

Underneath the platform, Whitney nearly bumped her head on one of the support beams at the sound of Stone's voice so near. "Hi, Stone. I'll be out in a minute."

There were sounds of metal against metal, then she slid out on a small board on wheels such as mechanics use to work under cars. She pushed herself up into a sitting position and glanced at Stone. He was wearing a well-cut tan suit, a crisp shirt, and a subdued tie. She, on the other hand, was covered from her neck to her old sneakers by a baggy pair of worn coveralls. A red bandana was rolled and tied around her head like a sweatband.

Stone looked her over. "Do you plan on going to the rehearsal looking like a reject from the sixties?"

Frowning, Whitney tossed his remark around in her mind for a few seconds, but it didn't do any good. "A rejected what?"

"Hippy," he clarified with a glowering expression.

Her hands slid over her hips. "You think I'm hippy?"

Either she didn't know what a hippy was or she was purposely deflecting his words. He shook his head and murmured, "Never mind."

Whitney gave him another long stare. "I didn't realize it was so late. I'll be with you in a minute."

He watched as she walked over to the table where

Melvin was examining a set of blueprints. Her shape-
less coveralls were not the type of clothing appropriate
for a wedding rehearsal in a church. Out of habit, he
glanced at his watch. It would to be cutting it fine if he
had to wait for her to go home and change her clothes.

She pointed to a section of the drawing in front of
Melvin. "I think the problem is with the lid of the shell.
It's too heavy the way it is."

"If we make it too light," Melvin said, "the wind could
blow it open and possibly break it off."

Stone was impatient. "Whitney!"

Startled, Whitney turned her head and saw Stone
scowling at her. "We're having a little problem with the
clam shell."

"We need to get going, Whitney, or we'll hold up the
rehearsal."

"We'll make it." She turned her attention back to
Melvin. "We could beef up the frame and use a material
to cover it that has a looser weave so the air could go
through it. Then the mechanics will be in control and
not the wind. We can explain to the committee that
they need to choose lightweight flowers to cover the
surface."

"It might work," Melvin muttered, and made a few
notes on the drawing in front of him.

Stone watched in horrified fascination as Whitney
began to lower the front zipper of her coveralls inch by
tantalizing inch as she continued to confer with Melvin. Was she going to undress in front of him and
Melvin? he wondered wildly. He was angry because she
was taking her clothes off in the presence of the other
man as if she did it all the time. An unfamiliar posses-
siveness streaked through him. He didn't want her
removing her clothes for anyone but him.

The zipper was open almost to her waist when Whitney finished her conversation with Melvin and walked over to a folding screen. She ducked behind it, and he could hear water running as she washed her hands. Then his imagination was fired by the sounds of cloth sliding over skin and zippers zipping. He needed to put some distance between himself and the screen for his sanity's sake. On the opposite side of the warehouse partitions had been erected to create a separate area for what appeared to be an office. There were two desks facing each other about ten feet apart, several filing cabinets, and two computer terminals. Behind each desk framed certificates hung on the partition, and Stone moved closer to read them.

On the first wall he saw Melvin Gunn's three diplomas stating his qualifications as an electrical engineer, along with a number of awards and letters of appreciation from various institutions and corporations. On the other side of the partition he found Whitney Grant's name on degrees in electrical engineering and computer design, along with her own awards and certificates of achievement.

The office space was surprisingly neat and orderly, considering the jumble and disorder in the work area. He let his experienced eye evaluate the way the area was set up. The lighting seemed adequate, but there was a great deal of wasted space between the various tables and benches. Tools were scattered around, requiring extra effort to get them.

While he waited for Whitney, Stone decided to use the time to learn a little more about how the two designers worked. He could already see several ways to advise them on making their workplace more productive with less waste of time, space, and effort. With that purpose in mind, he walked to where Whitney's partner sat hunched over the drawing board. Melvin hadn't displayed any great inclination to chat, but Stone was going to try to pry some information from him.

Behind the screen, Whitney slipped an aqua georgette dress over her head and pulled it down over her hips. She had worn the appropriate underclothes beneath her coveralls, so it didn't take long for her to change. For some idiotic reason, her fingers were unusually clumsy as they fumbled with the zipper. She stopped and held her hands out in front of her. Good Lord, she thought in stunned amazement. Her hands were actually shaking. Was she that nervous because Stone Hamilton was waiting for her?

While she was growing up, she had met diplomats, dignitaries, senators, and high-ranking military officers, and had never felt this strange tension, a confusing mixture of apprehension and exhilaration.

She could hear Stone's deep voice as he talked with Melvin. Anticipation swept over her as it had that morning when she'd woken up thinking about Stone. For the life of her she couldn't imagine why she was so preoccupied with a man who was a walking wristwatch.

Her reaction to Stone was too new to assess and analyze with any sense of proportion. He wasn't one of the animated creations she could manipulate and control. He was an unknown quantity of flesh and blood with a mind of his own. He was also the first man who disturbed her to the extent that she was rushing around like a deranged chicken.

She knew better than to think she could appeal to a man like Stone. The last man she had been interested in had told her she was as sexually responsive as one of her mechanical figures—when it was switched off. No, she told herself firmly, Stone Hamilton wouldn't be attracted to her personally. Remember, he was here only because Sylvia had asked him to escort her to the rehearsal at the church.

She slipped her stockinged feet into her heels, then walked over to the sink, using the mirror above it to apply a touch of makeup and brush her hair. Finally, taking a deep steadying breath, she walked around the screen. She saw Stone's tall figure leaning over the drawing table as Melvin pointed something out to him.

Taking advantage of the opportunity to study him without being observed, she noticed how the light over the drawing board highlighted the various shades of his thick blond hair. His suit fit him perfectly, accentuating his shoulders and slim hips, making her wonder about the man under the clothing. He carried himself with a lithe masculine grace that appealed to her, although she couldn't explain why she was attracted to this particular man. She just knew she was.

What in the world was wrong with her? she wondered frantically. If she didn't know better, she would think she had a bad case of raging hormones. This desire to rip a man's clothes off was something new and scary. It was odd how much pleasure she received from simply looking at him.

He didn't look up until she spoke. "I'm ready."

Stone turned his head and slowly straightened when he saw her. His gaze roamed over her, and his stomach tightened as though he had been punched. Even in his wildest imaginings, he would never have pictured her like this. She was beautiful. The color of her dress matched her eyes and the simplicity of its lines allowed him to appreciate her figure rather than admire the dress covering it. She had wisely stayed away from frills and ruffles, which would have been too fussy for her small frame.

Uncomfortable under his intent gaze, Whitney said, "If we don't leave now, we're going to be late."

The fact that Stone didn't even look at his watch, was no small indication of how the sight of her affected him. His gaze trailed down her shapely legs and back up to her face. His blood had heated with a fire that was reflected in the depths of his green eyes.

Whitney wasn't accustomed to having such blatant sexuality aimed in her direction, and when she spoke again her voice was laced with irritation. "What are you staring at?"

"You."

"Is my slip showing or something?"

He shook his head and gave her a crooked smile. "You dress up nicely, Miss Grant."

"Thank you, Mr. Hamilton." She flicked a glance at his fashionably cut suit. "May I admire your attire as well?"

"You may." He walked toward her and held out his arm. "Let's not waste all this finery on Melvin. He doesn't seem to notice anything but his blueprints. Shall we go?"

She took his arm. Over her shoulder, she said good-bye to Melvin, who casually raised his arm as he continued to concentrate on the designs in front of him.

"Is your partner usually so single-minded?" Stone asked with amusement as he opened the door. "All he talked about was his design for a fire-breathing dragon. At least I think that's what he was talking about. Your friend Nancy was right. He uses big words in a language I'm not familiar with."

"Melvin prefers automated beings to human beings."

As Whitney walked past him through the door, her hand accidentally brushed against his thigh. Stone gripped the edge of the door to keep from reaching for her. He closed his eyes briefly as her provocative scent drifted around him.

His extreme reaction to Whitney had thrown him off balance from the first moment he had seen her, and it wasn't getting any better. Actually, it had been from the first moment he had felt her slender, supple body under his. He couldn't understand it. Rarely did he allow anything or anyone to disrupt his orderly existence, yet from his first glance this unusual woman had gotten under his skin and in his blood.

If he made it through the evening without grabbing her, it was going to be a miracle.

During the drive to the church, Stone asked her the same questions he had asked Melvin. He fared a little better with Whitney.

"Do you and Melvin do the construction of the mechanized figures yourself?"

"Most of the time. It's easier to build a figure from the ground up than try to wire a figure already made."

"Am I right in assuming you work on more than one project at a time? Melvin was designing a dragon, which doesn't seem to go with the lobster and King Neptune."

"The dragon has been ordered for a display in Chinatown and the sea creatures are a mock-up for a float for the Rose Bowl Parade in Pasadena. We're doing only the basic designs of the animated figures."

"Do you do the costumes, too?"

She shook her head. "The costumes are made by professional seamstresses we have under contract. You met one yesterday."

"The lady from the children's store?"

Whitney nodded. "Nancy follows our rough sketches to design each costume and sews them herself, or subcontracts the designs out to someone else."

Stone slanted a glance at her. "How did you get into the business of designing mechanical figures?"

She heard the note of disbelief in his voice. She had heard that same tone from her father when she told him she was going to go into business with Melvin Gunn. She didn't like it then and she didn't like it now. What she did was perhaps a little unusual, but it was nothing to be ashamed of.

"I like it," she replied simply.

He was dissatisfied with her reply and dug further. "You mentioned deadlines. How much time do you have to complete a job?"

She shifted in the seat to look at him. "Why all these questions about my work?"

"I noticed the way you have your workshop laid out. There might be a more efficient way of arranging the area to save time. Especially if you operate under the pressure of deadlines, it would help to have your work area arranged for maximum productivity."

"Maybe time isn't as important to us as it is to you. We get the job done, and that's what's important."

"I was just going to suggest a few changes to help you work more—"

"Efficiently. Thanks all the same but we'll struggle along in our bumbling way." Changing the subject abruptly, she asked him how long he had known David, the groom.

Stone took the hint and backed off. "He was my roommate in college. How long have you known Sylvia?"

"Since high school in San Diego. Our fathers worked together." She glanced over at him. "It's funny you and I have never met before."

"San Francisco is a large city."

That wasn't what she meant and she had the feeling he knew it. The city was large, but David and Sylvia's circle of friends was relatively small. Mr. Efficiency probably didn't schedule much time for friends in his little book, she decided.

At the church, the rehearsal went smoothly. As usual, Sylvia's ability to organize a roomful of elementary-school students was in full force. Everyone stood where they were supposed to stand and said what they were supposed to say during the first run-through.

With everyone gathered around, Sylvia ticked off the items on her list of reminders to ensure everything would go smoothly on her wedding day. Each person was told again where he or she should be at what time, and Stone received extra instructions regarding Whitney.

"You will be sure to pick up Whitney in plenty of time to get to the church, won't you?" Sylvia asked.

Stone nodded but Sylvia pressed further. "I won't have time to chase her down, so I'm making you responsible for getting her to the wedding on time. I feel better knowing you'll be taking charge of Whitney, Stone. She sometimes forgets things."

"We'll both be there," he said with an edge of irritation in his voice. He glanced at Whitney to see how she was reacting to being treated like an eight-year-old, but her expression was passive.

Whitney really wasn't offended or surprised by Sylvia's comment. It was the truth. Even though she didn't purposely go out of her way to be late or forget appointments, there were occasions when she got so involved in her work that everything else was temporarily forgotten. Her friends understood that and accepted her the way she was. She wondered if Stone could.

If he couldn't, if he found her irresponsible and un-organized, he wasn't the only one, she reminded herself. Her father held the same opinion.

After the rehearsal, everyone went to dinner at a small restaurant that had been reserved for their party alone. There was a five-piece orchestra playing quietly during dinner and for dancing afterward. The food was delicious, the company enjoyable . . . and Stone never left Whitney's side. As best man, he considered accompanying Whitney his duty. As a man, he considered it a necessity.

They were sitting across from Sylvia's parents, and midway through the first course Mr. Bascomb looked over at Whitney.

"How is your father?" he asked.

If Stone hadn't been watching Whitney so closely, he would have missed the way her lips tightened briefly before she replied. "He's surviving retirement nicely, with a golf club in one hand and a pair of pruning shears in the other."

Mr. Bascomb chuckled. "I can't imagine Admiral Stewart Grant retired."

"I don't think Mother can either," Whitney said. "She's wondering what to do with a husband who's home all the time."

"We were sorry to hear they couldn't attend the wedding."

"They had a prior commitment."

"Are they still living in Fort Lauderdale?"

Whitney nodded, wondering how she could change the subject without being too obvious.

Mr. Bascomb, however, was perfectly content to talk about Admiral Grant. He recounted several experiences he'd had serving under the admiral aboard ship. Some were humorous and some were not, but Stone only half listened. He was still trying to assimilate the fact that Whitney's father was the spit-and-polish Admiral "Gung Ho" Grant.

The Admiral, who had been the commanding officer of the naval base in Alameda, on the other side of the bay, had received a fair amount of publicity in the past. Local newspapers and televison news programs were always carrying stories about his controversial actions. An exacting disciplinarian, he had instituted strict dress codes regarding uniforms, prohibiting beards or mustaches, and had even restricted certain types of bumper stickers on cars driven on the base. The admiral rode out the waves of protest without changing his course.

While Mr. Bascomb talked, Whitney was aware of the waiting stillness of the man next to her and could feel the curiosity emanating from him. Since they had arrived at the restaurant, Stone had remained glued to her side. She wondered if he was acting as her escort because Sylvia had asked him to, or whether he actually wanted to be with her.

At least he wasn't looking at his watch every few minutes, she thought, preoccupied with time like the rabbit in *Alice in Wonderland*. She would like to have checked his appointment book to see if he had made an entry for this evening. She imagined it would read: *Escort Miss Whitney Grant to wedding rehearsal from six-thirty to . . . ?* As organized as he was, he undoubtedly had added the time he would take her home when he had written down the time he would pick her up. She had never met anyone who was so intent on accounting for every minute of the day as Stone Hamilton. Except perhaps her father.

Her father's priorities were discipline and organization, and that had given her a distaste for a regimented life. Stone seemed to be as fanatical about efficiency and promptness as her father had always been. If she had any sense, she would stay as far away from Stone as she could. It was unfortunate that she thought he was the most intriguing man she had ever met.

After the waiters had removed the last of the dishes, Sylvia and David took to the dance floor first. Other members of the wedding party and their families gradually joined them. Whitney was content to watch until, much to her dismay, Mr. Bascomb brought up her father again. He still had the anchor firmly between his teeth and wasn't about to drop the subject of the U.S. Navy and Admiral Grant. Neither topic was what Whitney wanted to hear or discuss.

She didn't like it much when Mr. Bascomb brought her into the conversation either. "The last time I saw your father was two years ago when he came to San Francisco. I remember how upset he was when he learned about your business. He didn't consider designing those toy things a proper line of work. What are you doing now?"

Whitney smiled tightly. "I'm still designing those toy things."

She abruptly pushed back her chair and stood. Looking down at the man seated next to her, she asked, "Would you like to dance, Stone?"

Stone gazed up at her in surprise, noting the tension in the faint lines around her eyes and mouth. Holding Whitney in his arms on a dance floor wouldn't be one of his wiser moves, but he hadn't done anything particularly clever since he had found her under a pile of teddy bears. Besides, the chance to talk to her alone was too good to pass up. He took her hand as he stood up, excusing himself to the others seated at their table.

On the dance floor, he held out his arms and felt an odd tug in his chest when she stepped into them, bringing her slender body against his. All the questions he wanted to ask faded away as he absorbed her slight weight, her closeness as natural and right as breathing.

To try to take his mind off the tantalizing feel of her in his arms, he asked, "Would you have asked me to dance if you hadn't disliked the topic of conversation at our table?"

Whitney raised her eyes, surprised at his perception. She hadn't realized she had been so transparent. "My father is not my favorite choice of dinner conversation."

"I noticed," he said dryly.

For a minute they danced silently, taking the minimum number of steps. Then Stone asked, "Why did you let Mr. Bascomb get away with calling your mechanical figures toys? I haven't known you long, but I can't imagine your letting that remark go by so easily."

"Mr. Bascomb was only repeating what he had heard my father say."

"I was surprised to hear you're the daughter of 'Gung Ho' Grant."

Whitney gave a ghost of a laugh. "Most people are. Could we change the subject?"

"Why? From what I've read about him in the newspaper, he's quite an interesting man."

"The media have been known to occasionally distort facts."

"You mean your father isn't the strict disciplinarian he's made out to be?"

Whitney had had enough of talking about her father. "If I didn't care to discuss my father with Mr. Bascomb, what makes you think I want to talk about him with you? I would rather talk about the weather, the situation in the Middle East, or the price of pork bellies in the futures market than about Admiral Stewart Grant, Retired."

He loosened his hold enough to look down at her. "I don't think discussing pork bellies is the way to get to know each other better."

She gazed at him seriously. "Is that what we're doing?"

His hand on her waist tightened to hold her more securely against him. "That's what I'm doing."

She could feel his hard thighs move against hers, the slippery material of her dress creating a delicious friction between them. "That's not all you're doing. If any of my figures danced this close, I'd have to get an R rating for the display."

A corner of his mouth lifted slightly in amusement. "This isn't dancing," he murmured huskily. "This feels more like a mating ritual."

"Maybe it would be better if we returned to the table," she said quietly. "Listening to Mr. Bascomb recite my father's virtues would be more socially acceptable than having everyone question mine."

Stone chuckled. "I wasn't complaining, Whitney. I like being close to you. It's what I've wanted since the moment I met you."

Startled, she missed a step, and she clutched his shoulder as she struggled to retain her balance. "What a thing to say!"

"It's true." There was a note of bewilderment in his voice, as if although he admitted his desire, he didn't understand it. "I've wanted you from the second that last teddy bear was removed from between us."

"Stone," she began hesitantly. "If there are two people in San Francisco who have no business even thinking about getting involved, it's you and me. We have absolutely nothing in common."

"Oh, I wouldn't say that. I think we have something very basic in common." He sighed heavily. "But you're right. In any other way except physically, we would probably drive each other nuts."

Whitney agreed with him, and was unable to keep the regret she felt out of her voice. "It's just as well we realize it now before we do something really stupid."

"Right," he murmured. "It would be the dumbest move we could make."

She looked down. "I couldn't agree more."

She believed the words when she said them, but was surprised at the wrench of disappointment within her. Still, she was a realist. Wanting something didn't mean she could have it. And she did want him. Physically, emotionally, in all those strange ways a woman wanted a man. It had come upon her suddenly, unexpectedly, yet she recognized it for what it was, even though the feeling was unfamiliar.

The music changed to a fast tune, and Stone dropped his arms from around her. For a long moment, they stood still in the middle of the dance floor simply looking at each other.

Finally he spoke. "Do you want to go back to the table or are you ready to go home?"

Whitney didn't have to think about her answer. The evening was over as far as she was concerned. "I'd rather go home if you're ready to leave."

He was. Even though he had said what he wanted to say, he felt unsettled and restless. For a man who took great pains to run his life smoothly, he was finding the going a little rough since he had met Whitney.

It didn't get any better as he drove her home. It was a bumpy ride, and it had nothing to do with the surface of the road. Whitney chatted gaily about everything from the best restaurant in Chinatown to the unusually cool weather for that time of year. It was as though silence was an enemy she had to combat by chattering nonstop.

Stone was ready to tell her to forget everything he had said earlier on the dance floor when she interrupted her own discourse on the weather. "You're going the wrong way."

"How can I be going the wrong way? This is the way to the warehouse."

"That's not where I live. That's where I work."

Summoning up the last reserves of his patience, he said, "All right, Whitney. Where do you live?"

She gave him directions and he followed them silently, eventually pulling up in front of a tall apartment building in a nice area of the city.

Whitney hesitated for a moment with her hand on the door latch. "Would you like to come in for coffee?"

He shook his head. "No," he said more harshly than he had intended. If he came in with her, he wasn't sure he would be able to leave until morning. It was best the way it was.

He ignored the blank stare he was receiving, aware that his rough reply had hurt her, even though she managed to hide it. He didn't know how he knew what she was feeling, but he did. Perhaps because it was an echo of his own emotions.

"Where should I pick you up on Saturday before the wedding?" he asked, "Here or the warehouse?"

"Here," she said softly.

"Fine."

She smiled faintly. "I'll be ready this time."

He knew her better now. "I won't take a chance. I'll call you before I come."

Whitney's smile faded. He was pointing out how irresponsible she was about time, and she didn't need their differences pointed out to her. She knew what they were. "All right," she murmured.

"Whitney," he said quietly. "This is the sensible thing to do."

She knew he was referring to their earlier agreement to end their relationship before it even began. They were oil and water. They couldn't mix.

She nodded, then opened her door and walked toward the entrance of her apartment building, her spine straight and rigid, her eyes sad and resigned.

Stone watched her as she pushed open the glass door and vanished at the far end of the lobby. He sat in his car staring at the building, unable to leave as he fought the urge to go after her.

Finally he shifted gears and drove away.

Three

Melvin was still sitting at the drawing table when Whitney returned to the warehouse an hour after Stone had left her at her apartment. The lamp hanging over his table glinted off the thick lenses of his glasses as he looked up at her. She had on jeans and a bulky sweater instead of the dress she had worn when she left the warehouse earlier.

"Where's Prince Charming?"

"Charming someone else," she said flatly. She set the box she had brought with her down on the workbench near Melvin's table. "Do you want some pizza?"

He pushed his lanky frame off the stool. "Sure."

With her hands on either side of her, she hefted herself up onto the workbench. Her feet dangled over the side as she helped herself to one of Pepé's thick slices of pizza. Stopping at Pepé's hadn't been such a good idea since Pepé had immediately begun teasing her about her "fella" while she waited for the pizza. Just because Stone was the only man beside Melvin that Pepé had ever seen her with was no reason for Pepé to go on and on, she thought with irritation.

Melvin sat on the bench on the other side of the pizza box and for a few minutes they ate in companionable silence.

After his third slice of pizza, Melvin said, "If it weren't for you and Pepé's pizzas, I would probably starve."

"Maybe we should program one of the machines to automatically serve us food, since we keep forgetting to eat."

Melvin chuckled. "We could design a plump grandmother-type figure wearing an apron to nag us every five hours or so. She could hold an apple pie in one hand and a big wooden spoon in the other."

Whitney gazed around the large interior of the warehouse, wondering how it had looked through Stone's eyes. "Maybe we should simply get a clock. Then we would know when it was time to eat and to sleep."

"I thought we decided we didn't need a clock. We agreed this wasn't going to be a nine-to-five operation when we started, remember? The whole reason we began our own business is because we didn't want anyone telling us what to make on an assembly-line basis."

"Have you ever thought we could be more . . . efficient?" She struggled with that last word, but it was the only one that fit.

Melvin laid his half-eaten slice of pizza back into the box and concentrated all his attention on Whitney. "What we do can't be done in a standardized set amount of time, Whitney. You know that. Some projects take longer than others, especially if it calls for a lot of figures and if we're having problems. I thought our main purpose was to design animated figures for displays, not to watch a clock."

"Have you ever thought that what we do is strange?"

"Nope," he replied easily. "I let other people worry about that."

She jumped down from the workbench and walked over to the drawing board. "Did you get the glitch with the dragon worked out?"

"Just about." He eased his long body off the work-bench and joined her in front of his table. "What's wrong, Whitney?"

She picked up several blueprints and stared blindly at them. "I don't know. Maybe I've got a late case of spring fever."

Melvin shook his head. "What you got is a case of overexposure to Prince Charming. What did he say? That someone who looks like one of the figures on a wedding cake shouldn't be monkeying around with tools?"

Whitney gave him a sour look. "I'm not that tiny. And leave Prince—Stone out of this."

Melvin took the papers from her and laid them back down on the table. Slouching again on the stool, he said, "I'd be happy to leave him out as long as he doesn't interfere in Grant and Gunn Animations."

"He won't. The only reason he came for me tonight was to escort me to the wedding rehearsal. He's in charge of making sure I get to the wedding on Saturday and then I'll never see him again."

Her partner looked up. "How do you feel about that?"

She shrugged. "Having the best man escort the maid of honor is Sylvia's idea of making sure I'll be there on time."

"I mean about never seeing Prince Charming again."

"It means I won't be seeing him again," she said flatly. "Unless we have more mutual friends who end up getting married which is highly unlikely." She started toward the screen where she had left her coveralls. "I'm going to change and get to work on that clam shell."

Melvin stared at her for a long moment, then yawned. "Well, you're on your own. I'm going home."

"Okay. See you tomorrow."

Whitney disappeared behind the screen and lifted her coveralls off the hook she had hung them on earlier. She was stepping into them when she heard Melvin clear his throat.

She stuck her head around the edge of the screen. "I thought you were leaving. Did you forget something?"

Melvin shifted from one foot to the other, looking exceedingly awkward and uncomfortable. "Ah, is there anything you want to talk about?"

"No," she said, surprised, "there's nothing I want to talk about. Go on home, Melvin."

When he still hesitated, she smiled. "I'm fine. There're a few things I want to do here tonight, that's all."

He didn't look thoroughly convinced, but he nodded and turned off the light over his table. "I'll see you later."

As she zipped up the front of her coveralls, she heard the steel door close loudly behind Melvin. Coming out from behind the screen, she stood for a minute and looked around the wide open space. When she crossed over to her desk her footsteps sounded unusually loud and hollow. She sat down heavily in her old leather chair and leaned back, ignoring the creaking protest of the worn springs.

What in the world was she doing here? she wondered wearily. It was after midnight and she was alone in a dark, drafty warehouse. She had used the excuse to

Melvin and to herself that she wanted to work, but she had never felt less like picking up a tool.

She raised her gaze to the framed certificates hanging on the wall. For all her education, she was incredibly stupid. She could design, construct, and operate a mechanical figure to dance the highland fling or sing "The Star-Spangled Banner." She could program a computer to do anything she wanted it to do. She could turn flat pieces of metal into believable facsimiles of animals, birds, and people.

But she was dumb enough to be attracted to a man who didn't want anything to do with her. They were exact opposites . . . except for a strange physical affinity which merely complicated things.

If only she could program her emotions so she didn't remember the feel of his warm hand on her back and the glide of his thighs against hers as they danced. When she had walked into his arms on the dance floor, she had known it was where she wanted to be.

But he was a man who preferred to live a regulated life, each minute carefully planned and jotted down in his appointment book. No entries for extracurricular activities involving a woman who never knew what time it was . . . or cared.

A little before noon the following day, Stone was sitting at his desk and debating about going to get something to eat. His secretary hadn't scheduled anything for him for the next hour, but he wasn't hungry.

He stared out the window. He didn't want to go to a restaurant. What he wanted was to get some sleep, or rather, to recover the sleep he had lost last night because he couldn't stop thinking about Whitney Grant.

No, he corrected that thought. What he wanted was to see her again.

It was the last thing he should do, but it was the only thing he wanted to do. It was crazy, yet he needed to see her. Needed to touch her. There were a lot of things he wanted to do with her, but right now he would settle for just seeing her.

Thoughts of her kept intruding when he tried to shut them out. No matter how many times he told himself to forget about her, it didn't do any good. She was there deep inside him, regardless of how hard he tried to shut her out.

An hour later, he gave up. He got out his appointment book and looked up the number she had given him at Pepé's Pizza, the number at the warehouse.

Whitney didn't answer the phone. Melvin did.

Recognizing the other man's abrupt voice, Stone asked, "Is Whitney there?"

"No, she isn't," Melvin said testily. "Who's this?"

"Stone Hamilton. Do you know when she'll be back?"

There was a short pause on the line, and then Melvin said, "Who knows? She just called to tell me she can't get her car started. She used the last of her change in a pay phone and doesn't have any cash to take a taxi. She asked me to come and get her in Union Square. Do you want me to tell her to call you when she gets back?"

Stone frowned. He didn't want to talk to her on the phone. He wanted to see her. On impulse, he volunteered to get her. "I'm not that far away from Union Square. Have you called anyone to fix her car?"

"Not yet. I was about to do that when you called."

"I'll take care of it and bring her back to the warehouse."

Melvin didn't debate the issue. "I told her to wait for me in front of the St. Francis Hotel and not to wander off somewhere. But with Whitney, I can't guarantee she'll be there."

"I'll find her."

"Thanks, Prince. I really appreciate it."

The line went dead and Stone stared at the receiver as if something was wrong with it. He could have sworn Whitney's partner had called him Prince. Shaking his head, he put the phone down. He must have been hearing things.

Checking the appointment calendar on his desk, he saw all he had down for the afternoon was a consultation with some members of his staff. The meeting would probably last a couple of hours and could be postponed. The paperwork waiting for him could also wait a little longer.

As he walked through the outer office, he told his secretary to notify the others there wouldn't be a meeting until later.

"Are you all right?" Mrs. Taylor asked.

He smiled at the astonished expression on the woman's usually placid face. Using the phrase Whitney had thrown at him, he said, "It's not the end of the world if I change my schedule, Mrs. Taylor."

Flustered, the older woman answered, "It's just that you never have before."

His secretary's words came back to Stone as he drove toward Union Square. He couldn't blame Mrs. Taylor for being so surprised. The only time he had ever canceled any appointments was when he had the flu and had been unable to get out of bed. Other than that, he had never deviated from his normal routine. Since meeting Whitney, though, he hadn't felt normal or routine.

After his stupid speech about not getting involved with her, he had a feeling there was going to be one more woman who thought he was crazy. Maybe he was.

When he arrived at Union Square, he didn't have to go looking for Whitney. That was a good thing since parking spaces were at a premium in downtown San Francisco. He recognized her immediately, even though she was wearing large sunglasses. Dressed in an over-sized white shirt worn over a flowing matching skirt with a woven belt tied at her waist, Whitney was standing in front of the elegant hotel, holding several shopping bags at her side. A slight breeze tousled her dark curls and sent her skirt waving gently against her tanned legs.

He pulled his car over to the curb in front of the hotel. It would be worth his life to get out of it in the heavy traffic. He lowered the electric window and leaned across the seat to call to her.

At the sound of her name, Whitney looked around, but she couldn't see Melvin or the van anywhere. Then she heard her name again, accompanied by the honking of a horn, and her eyes widened when she recognized the BMW and the man driving it. She walked over to Stone's car and bent down to his window to stare at him with wide, surprised eyes.

"Get in," he ordered.

She was tempted but she had to turn down his offer. "I'm waiting for Melvin to pick me up."

"He's not coming." He reached over and opened the door. "If you want a ride back to the warehouse, you have to get in the car."

Whitney didn't move, and the driver of the car behind Stone's impatiently pounded on his horn.

"We could stay here and discuss this," Stone said in a calm, unhurried voice, "but the guy behind me wants to get where he's going sometime today."

She pushed the car door open farther with her elbow and started to get in, but the shopping bags inhibited her progress.

"Hand me the bags," Stone said, "and I'll put them in the back seat."

She thrust a bag at him as she slid onto the seat, bumping into his outstretched hand. Several tissue-wrapped items spilled out onto his lap. Looking down, Stone saw pale pink wisps of silk and lace draped over his thighs. Completely oblivious to the horn of the car behind him, he picked up the tantalizing bits of feminine clothing.

"Nice," he murmured, imagining how the frothy garment would feel against Whitney's skin.

She snatched the nightgown out of his hand. "I hope Sylvia thinks so. This is her wedding present."

"Lucky David." He gave the man behind them a break and put the car in gear as soon as Whitney shut the door.

Ignoring his last remark, Whitney folded the nightgown, rewrapped it in the tissue paper, and placed it back in its bag. To get the shopping bags out of the way, she put them on the back seat. "Why are you here instead of Melvin?" she asked at last.

"I wanted to see you," he said easily, then added, "Fasten your seat belt."

"Why?"

"Haven't you heard? It's for safety's sake."

"I meant why do you want to see me?"

She wasn't going to make it easy for him, he thought, but then he couldn't really blame her after what he had said last night. "Let me put it another way. I have to see you whether I want to or not. The choice seems to be taken out of my hands." Flicking a quick glance at her, he added, "I could see you better without those glasses."

She reached up and removed the sunglasses. Her gaze fell on his hands gripping the steering wheel, and she remembered how good his hands had felt holding her. Giving herself a mental shake, she forced her mind back to what he had said about choices. "We all make choices every day. Some are easier to make and to accept than others. I accepted the choice you made last night." She took a deep breath. "And I think you were right. We shouldn't get involved. We're too different. We'd be miserable."

A light had turned red, and Stone was able to look at her rather than the road. "I decided I would rather be miserable with you than without you."

She felt she was being tugged in opposite directions—the one she wanted to go and the one she should go. Her mind told her their earlier agreement to stay uninvolved was the smart one, but her body screamed that she should take the chance he was offering to see what they might find together.

Her mind won the battle. "It would make more sense if we left it the way it was."

He chuckled. "Sense doesn't have anything to do with what's between us, Whitney. If it did, Melvin would be driving you back to the warehouse. What I'm suggesting is that we get to know each other. Maybe our differences aren't as diverse as we originally thought."

The light changed and he returned his attention to his driving. Whitney was silent for several blocks, then she said softly, "I don't think I would be very good at getting involved with you or anyone."

"Why not?"

"Until I was eighteen, I lived under a strict, dictatorial regime where I had to answer to someone else for the smallest detail. When I left home, I vowed never to be answerable to anyone but myself. I don't want to be accountable to anyone for what I do, where I go, and who I am. So you see, I wouldn't be the one for you to have a relationship with."

"Hmm, I see your problem." He turned a corner and drove down the street where the warehouse was located.

"I didn't say it was a problem. I'm just telling you why we shouldn't get involved."

He parked in front of the warehouse and shut off the engine. Shifting slightly, he placed his arm casually on the back of the seat and gave her his whole attention. "You're telling me why we shouldn't but not why we should."

"The shouldn'ts outweigh the shoulds," she said, disregarding the finer aspects of grammar.

Suddenly he brought his hand down and held it palm up in front of her.

She looked at his hand and then up at his face. "What?" She glanced down at his hand again. "Am I supposed to pay for the ride?"

"No. The ride's on me. I want you to put your hand in mine."

"Why?" she asked suspiciously.

"To prove a point." When she still looked askance at his hand, he prompted, "Go ahead. It's clean, I swear."

Chewing her lip, she lifted her hand and placed it tentatively on top of his. "Now what?"

His fingers closed around her small hand. Her eyes

snapped up to meet his as a current of heat flowed from his hand to hers. His smile was very male and very knowing. "This definitely comes under the heading of shoulds. This doesn't happen all that often. In fact, I don't remember ever feeling this before. It's like an uncontrollable flood, sweeping me along toward you. All we have to do is learn to swim together."

"Or sink."

"I'm a good swimmer, Whitney."

"I'm not sure I am."

"Let's find out."

His fingers tightened on her hand to draw her toward him, his other hand going to the nape of her neck. His thumb lifted her chin as he lowered his head to claim her mouth.

The extent of his hunger should have startled her, but it didn't. It merely echoed her own. A fiery glow began to seep through her, growing in intensity when he slanted his mouth over hers to deepen the kiss. It seemed to go on and on, into eternity and beyond.

A shuddering breath escaped her when he moved to sample the taste of her neck, and Stone felt his control slip dangerously at that sound of her arousal.

Lifting his head, he stared down at her, fascinated by the way she slowly opened her eyes and met his with honesty and a hint of vulnerability. A man could fall into those blue depths and never wish to be rescued.

Her pink tongue stroked across her bottom lip to savor the taste of him lingering there.

"Whitney," he murmured, groaning softly. "Don't do that. I've never heard of anyone drowning in a BMW, but if I kiss you again, I'll be in over my head."

"I think I already am," she said, a slight catch in her voice.

A corner of his mouth curved into a soft smile. His arms went around her to comfort her and because he wanted to feel her against him one more time. Then he moved back behind the steering wheel, one hand remaining on her shoulder.

The sound of the metal door sliding open drew his gaze away from her, and he saw Melvin's thin figure standing in the doorway. He made an impatient gesture with his hand that was obviously meant for Whitney. Nodding in Melvin's direction, Stone said regretfully, "I think you're being paged."

Whitney turned her head and saw Melvin wave again with urgency for her to come inside. She looked back at Stone. "I'd better go."

He slid back his sleeve and checked the time. "I need to get back to work too. Tell me where you left your car and I'll get a mechanic to fix it."

"You don't need to do that, Stone. I can—"

"I know you can," he interrupted. "So can I."

"Melvin has probably already called someone."

"I told him I would take care of it. What kind of car do you drive?"

Melvin was still waiting for her, his expression growing more and more impatient. "It's a black Volkswagen Rabbit." She told him where it was parked, gave him the license number, and handed him her keys. "I don't know why I'm letting you do this."

He reached into the back for her shopping bags and handed them to her. "Will you be here later?"

"I don't know. Later isn't here yet."

He stared at her as if wondering what she was talking about. "That's how I am, Stone," she said. "I don't plan each day down to the last minute. I've been trying to tell you that."

"And I've been trying to tell you it doesn't matter." He muttered something under his breath, then said, "I won't be able to see you tonight after all. I just remembered David's stag party is tonight."

A teasing glint flashed in her eyes. "Dancing girls jumping out of cakes?"

"I doubt it. Sylvia probably made all the arrangements."

He leaned over and kissed her lightly. "You'd better go see what Melvin wants before he waves his arm off. Think about what I said."

Whitney spent the rest of the afternoon doing very little else except thinking about what Stone had said. The emergency that had Melvin in a panic was that the float committee was coming to check on the progress of the marine designs that afternoon. Even while talking to the committee members and explaining each creation, Whitney found it impossible to block out thoughts of Stone completely.

After the designs were approved with only a few minor changes to be made, Melvin settled down at his computer. As Whitney sat back in her chair she remembered the odd fascination and curiosity in Stone's eyes when she had talked about her work. She had seen something else in his eyes, too. An awareness of her as a woman, a desirable woman. She still wasn't sure they had anything in common other than a powerful physical attraction.

Irritated with herself and the situation, Whitney forced her concentration back to her work.

Around five o'clock, her car was returned by a mechanic who explained how minor the problem had been as he handed her a sizable bill. She wrote a check and sent him on his way. Her previous experiences with car repair companies were of long waits and huge charges. Her car had been repaired quickly and she knew she had Stone to thank for somehow getting the mechanic out immediately.

A simple thank you didn't seem enough. If he had come to the warehouse along with her car, she could have thanked him in person. There was always the telephone, but calling him didn't appeal to her. There had to be some other way to let him know she appreciated his taking the time to arrange for her car to be repaired. His time was valuable to him and he had used some of it on her.

Suddenly she grinned and walked over to a large metal cabinet along one wall of the warehouse. There she found exactly what she wanted.

Four

The first indication Stone had that something was disrupting his office staff the following morning was the sound of astonished laughter filtering through his closed door. Unless his next appointment was a juggling act, there was no reason for his usually sedate staff to be gathering in the outer office for a party. He pushed his chair back, walked around his desk, and opened the door.

His secretary, his receptionist, and most of the rest of the staff were standing in a circle looking down at something. One of the doormen was also in the group, joining in with the laughter and the various comments made about the object of their amusement.

"Where did it come from?" Stone heard Carl Chamber ask.

"Isn't it cute?" the receptionist said.

"My grandson would love this," Mrs. Taylor added.

Stone came up behind Carl and asked, "What's going on?"

Carl stood to one side so Stone could see what they were all exclaiming over. "You have to see it to believe it."

Stone looked down and his mouth fell open in astonishment. Standing on the floor was a two-foot-high, white, furry, mechanical rabbit dressed in a red jacket and plaid waistcoat. He held an oversized plastic watch in one paw, and his head moved as he looked down at the watch and then up to gaze from side to side. It was a replica of the rabbit from *Alice in Wonderland*, the rabbit who fretted constantly about being late.

Glancing quickly around at the others, Stone searched for one particular person. When he didn't see her, he asked, "How did this get here?"

The doorman supplied the answer. "A taxi driver delivered it to the desk downstairs. He was laughing his head off 'cause the rabbit was doing this during the whole ride. Since it was so heavy, I carried it up."

Stone's secretary handed him a folded sheet of paper sealed with a dab of red wax. "This came with it."

He broke the seal and unfolded the note. He read: *"It's time to thank you for getting my car fixed. Whitney."*

Mrs. Taylor saw his broad smile and asked, "Is it a gift from a client?"

"No, it isn't from a client," he said, chuckling.

He bent down and searched for a switch to turn off the rabbit, finally finding the control lever under the rabbit's waistcoat in the back. There were sounds of disappointment from those around him when the rabbit stopped moving. He started to pick it up, and was unprepared for how heavy it was. He didn't like the thought of Whitney lugging this heavy rabbit around by herself—and was startled by the possessive feeling, as though he had the right to try to protect her from doing anything that might hurt her.

Hefting Whitney's bunny up off the floor, he looked around at his staff. "Show's over."

Everyone returned to their work, still chuckling over the unusual break in their routine. Stone carried the rabbit into his office and sat it on the long, low credenza in front of the large window behind his desk. When he had switched off the rabbit, the head was in the upright position, its wide pink eyes staring up at Stone.

Meeting the rabbit's blank gaze, he said aloud, "You'll just have to wait here until I can take you back to your creator."

The rabbit stared mutely back at him and Stone groaned. "Lord, now she's got me talking to a stuffed bunny."

Shaking his head in exasperation, Stone returned to his chair with his back to the mechanical figure. He would have liked to return the rabbit to Whitney right away, but he had a full schedule of appointments. He'd have to wait until tonight. He decided to keep the note and slipped it under a paperweight on his desk.

If any of his clients thought it peculiar to see a large rabbit in the office of the efficiency expert, they didn't say anything. Occasionally their gaze shifted from Stone to the figure behind him, but no questions were asked. After all, this was San Francisco where the unusual was usual.

Every time his secretary brought in letters to be signed or contracts to go over, she glanced at the rabbit and smiled. There was an unusual amount of traffic into his office by various members of his staff the rest of the day. A few businessmen and women from some of the other offices in the building popped in to see the rabbit perform too. Stone lost count of the number of times he operated the switch to make the rabbit do his thing. The doorman had spread the word about the bizarre visitor in The Hamilton and Associates office.

When Mrs. Taylor was ready to leave for the day, she appeared once again in the doorway of his office to ask if there was anything he needed before she left.

"No, thank you, Mrs. Taylor. Good night."

The older woman hesitated and then asked, "Mr. Hamilton, is the rabbit going to stay?"

He knew Mrs. Taylor was dying to know why the rabbit was there in the first place and who had sent it. Coupled with his dashing out of the office the previous day, the rabbit no doubt confirmed her opinion that her boss was suddenly acting very oddly.

"Sorry, Mrs. Taylor. The rabbit has to go back to its hutch."

She blinked several times in surprise. "I thought perhaps the rabbit was going to be the office mascot or something."

Stone had to disappoint her. "I'm afraid not. I got some pretty strange looks from our clients this afternoon. He has to go back to Whitney's Wonderland."

"Don't you mean Alice's Wonderland?"

Turning his chair to enable him to see the rabbit, he studied the blank pink eyes staring at him. "Not in this case. This one definitely belongs to Whitney." Looking again at the woman still standing in the doorway, he smiled. "Good night, Mrs. Taylor."

The older woman nodded her head abruptly and shut his door, clearly at a loss as to what had come over her usually sedate, serious employer.

*　　*　　*

As Whitney stepped into the shower in her apartment, she was unaware that Stone was pounding on the metal door of the warehouse at that very moment. All day she had expected to hear from him after she had sent him the rabbit, but he hadn't come to the warehouse or phoned. She frowned as the water pelted down on her. Sending him the rabbit had seemed like a good idea at the time. She didn't see how he could have been insulted, but then again maybe he didn't think it was an appropriate way to say thank you.

He might consider the rabbit a silly messenger, yet he needed a bit of silliness in his life. In her opinion, he took life too seriously, believing time was to be filled instead of used for the pure pleasure of living.

She stepped out of the shower and grabbed a towel to wrap around her wet hair. Taking another towel, she dried herself off, then slipped her arms in a fleecy white robe and tied the belt around her waist. As she looked up, her eyes met her reflection in the mirror above the sink and she saw disappointment mixed with exhaustion.

She turned away in disgust with herself and left the bathroom. There wasn't anything she could do about the disappointment, but there was something she could do about the lack of sleep. She had left the warehouse with the sole purpose of going home to bed. She was going to have an early night to catch up on the sleep she had lost while wasting her time thinking about Stone Hamilton.

In the kitchen she poured some milk into a saucepan. While the milk was heating, she removed the towel from her head and rubbed her hair to dry it, not particularly concerned how it looked since there wasn't anyone around but her. She draped the damp towel over the back of a chair and walked over to a cupboard to get down the can of chocolate.

As she was prying off the lid, the doorbell rang. She quickly removed the pan off the burner before the milk boiled over, then pulled the lapels of her robe together as she went to answer the door. It was probably dear, sweet old Mr. Grandy, she thought. He seemed to have a sixth sense that told him when she was home. She wondered what he would ask to borrow this time. She knew he used the pretense of needing sugar, coffee, or milk just to have someone to talk to for a little while, and she didn't have the heart to refuse him a few minutes of company.

She opened the door expecting to see the kindly face of her neighbor, and her mouth dropped open when she saw instead Stone holding her rabbit in his arms as though it was a child. The rabbit's control switch was on and its head was bowing and turning.

She looked up at Stone and smiled faintly. "I should have included instructions on how to turn him off."

He switched off the rabbit. "I found it. If I hadn't my office staff would still be playing with it." He tilted his head slightly to one side as he looked down at her. "Can we come in?"

Whitney didn't immediately answer. She was oddly reluctant to let him into her apartment, although she couldn't come up with a valid reason why he shouldn't.

Stalling, she asked, "What time is it?"

He glanced at his watch. "A little after seven."

"I was getting ready for bed."

Stone didn't make the obvious remark about how early it was. Instead he stood with the rabbit in his arms, a faint smile on his lips, showing no apparent signs of taking the hint to leave.

Years of training under her mother's strict rules of politeness had her stepping back to allow him into the apartment.

Her heart skipped like a flat stone on a still lake as he stepped close to her in the foyer. It was the first time she had seen him in casual clothes instead of a suit. Black trousers, black shirt, and a black leather jacket emphasized his light hair and lean frame.

"I was making some hot chocolate," she said. "Would you like a cup? I don't have anything stronger."

"Fine," he said. He didn't particularly like hot chocolate, but his mind wasn't really on what she was offering. Still carrying the rabbit, he stepped from the foyer into the wide, open space on his right.

Her living room was a revelation. He didn't know what he expected but this wasn't it. The furnishings were an eclectic mixture of styles in dark green and white. The sofa and two matching chairs were covered in a subtle flowered print. They were arranged on a dark green carpet along with mahogany end tables and a large square mahogany table in front of the sofa. One wall was covered with white drapes, opened partway to reveal a floor-to-ceiling window that displayed a spectacular view of the San Francisco Bay and part of the skyline.

The room's main purpose was comfort with a side benefit of being pleasing to the eye. He knew that the furniture, the paintings, the plants, the books on the table were all there because Whitney liked them, not because of current trends or styles. This was her home.

He set the rabbit down on the chair nearest him,

then shrugged out of his jacket and laid it over the upholstered back of the same chair. His attention was drawn to a collection of Oriental fans displayed on the white wall behind the sofa. He didn't take the time to count them, but figured there were at least twenty of them. Of various sizes, they were fanned out to show their painted designs. Each fan was beautiful on its own but all together the collection was remarkable.

"Some of these fans look very old," he said, leaning closer to examine one of them.

"They are," she said. "I've been collecting them for a long time. They're part of my legacy from my days as a navy brat."

He turned to face her. "I like your home, Whitney," he said sincerely. "How long have you lived here?"

"About a year." She debated dashing into her bedroom to change into something more appropriate than her robe, but before she could excuse herself, Stone was speaking again.

"Your rabbit caused quite a stir in my office today. Practically everybody in the building came in to see him."

"You didn't have to bring him back. I sent him to you as a gesture of thanks."

"What would Melvin say if you gave away your inventory? This little guy is too expensive to accept as a gift. He belongs to you." He paused. "I'll keep the note, though."

Disturbed by the effect his husky voice had on her, Whitney said nothing as she walked back to the kitchen. A bar extended partway on one side of the living room, dividing it from the kitchen. Two stools were placed on each side of the counter, and Stone pulled out one on the living room side and sat down.

He watched her pour more milk into a saucepan on the stove. As she bent down to adjust the flame under the pan, he caught a brief, tantalizing glimpse of bare leg when her robe gaped open. All too soon, she straightened up and the robe fell closed once again. A heavy, throbbing desire hardened his body as he wondered if she was naked under the robe.

He had to clear his throat, which had become as tight as his control. "Did I interrupt your bath?"

She shook her head. "I had just finished." She leaned back against a counter and faced him. "I was getting ready to go to bed."

He had heard her the first time when she'd said that at the door, and he still didn't take the hint. "It's a little early to be going to bed, isn't it?"

"Not if you're tired."

"Or if you're not alone," he said, smiling as his gaze slowly slid down to the neckline of her robe.

If there was ever a time to change the subject, this was it. "How was the stag party?"

His reply was one short word. "Loud."

She could practically feel the heat of his gaze as it seemed to stroke her skin, moving from her breasts to her throat and finally to her face. She crossed her arms in front of her, slipping her hands into the sleeves of her robe so he wouldn't see them trembling. She felt oddly vulnerable and exposed in her robe, knowing he was fully aware she wore nothing underneath.

She attempted to keep her voice steady as she grasped at conversational straws. "David has a lot of friends."

He nodded. "And we were all there. About twenty guys arrived and toasted David's marriage in the time-honored tradition. Several had to be poured into taxis at the end of the evening. As stag parties go, I suppose it was a success."

"I thought there was usually entertainment of some kind, scantily dressed ladies who parade around as a reminder of what the groom is giving up. No lady jumping out of a cake?"

"Afraid not. Just two so-called brides who started out wearing wedding gowns and ended up wearing very little." Stone's mouth curved into a teasing smile. "Does that restore your illusions about stag parties?"

"Somewhat." She couldn't remain idle under his gaze. Turning toward the counter, she lifted the lid off a ceramic cookie jar in the shape of a fat goose head and removed a handful of cookies.

"I hope you like chocolate chip cookies," she said as she arranged them on a small plate. "I made them last night." Actually, she had baked them at about three in the morning when she couldn't sleep, but she wasn't about to tell him that.

His next remark was totally unexpected. "Whitney Grant, you're a phony."

She almost dropped the lid. Whipping her head around, she gasped, "What?"

"You're a complete phony. You pretend to be a non-conformist in your choice of career and the way you dress, but you come back to a warm, charming home straight out of *Good Housekeeping*. You even bake cookies. The mechanical engineer who wears coveralls, red suspenders, and grungy tennis shoes doesn't live here." His gaze shifted to the soft robe she was wearing. "This is where you allow yourself to be a woman, one who likes comfort and style around her."

It was what she had feared when she had hesitated

to let him enter her apartment. She had used her unusual work as a defense against getting involved with Stone, but now he had seen the way she lived, and he obviously approved.

"What were you expecting?" she asked tartly. "A dingy garage furnished with orange crates?"

He chuckled. "I'm learning not to take anything about you for granted. You have more sides than a multifaceted diamond. It's going to be interesting discovering each one of them."

It required an unusual amount of concentration to stir chocolate into the milk. "You may be disappointed. Some of those sides could be flawed."

"I hope so. Perfection is rare and usually uncomfortable to cope with."

It was Whitney's turn to be amused. "I don't think either one of us has to worry about perfection." She poured the fragrant hot chocolate into two mugs, then plopped several miniature marshmallows in each one. "Although you do try for perfection."

"Do I?"

She set the mugs down on the bar, then fetched the chocolate chip cookies and set them down as well.

"Isn't that why you chose to be an efficiency expert?" she asked. "Because you want the world to run as smoothly and as perfectly as possible?"

Stone looked down at the melting marshmallows and wondered how in hell he was going to swallow any of the sticky sweet drink. He raised his gaze to hers, and his mouth twisted with irony. "If I wanted my life to run smoothly, I wouldn't be here with you."

Whitney gave him a pained smile. "You didn't answer my question. Why did you choose to become an efficiency expert?" She held up one hand to stop him from answering. "I bet I know. Your father is a watchmaker."

"I don't know what he is," he replied frankly. "I don't even know who he is. I doubt if my mother does either."

Her eyes widened in shock, shame tinting her cheeks. "I'm sorry, Stone. It was a lousy attempt at a joke."

He shrugged. "Don't worry about it. To answer your question, I decided on a career in time management after years of living a hand-to-mouth existence. My mother was what used to be called a hippy in the sixties. We lived for a number of years in various lofts in the Haight–Ashbury district where she made jewelry to sell at flea markets, on the streets, and at craft shows. She didn't believe in worrying about tomorrow. It was going to arrive whether she planned for it or not."

Shock was replaced by a curious insight. "But you loved her anyway."

He nodded, smiling faintly. "I loved her anyway. Even when I had to steal money out of the cashbox she kept in a kitchen drawer so I could pay the rent. Or when I had to find homes for kittens and puppies she brought home and promptly forgot about. Having the electricity cut off was a common occurrence. She would stuff the bills in a drawer and forget she ever saw them."

"Where is she now?"

"I don't know," he said without a trace of emotion. "I went away to college at the University of California in Berkeley, and when I came back during the first semester break, she was gone."

"She just went away?" Whitney asked, a touch of anger in her voice. "Without telling you where she was going?"

"She liked to think she was a free spirit. The only thing I can honestly say she showed any sense of responsibility for was me. She could forget the pets she would bring home and the men she would be involved with as soon as they were out of sight, but she did take care of me in her own fashion. Once I went to college, she simply moved on."

Whitney found his past unbelievable, yet she believed him. It explained so much. His upbringing had been responsible for his desire to lead a structured, secure life as an adult. "Now I understand why you were cautious about getting involved with me. The night you picked me up at the warehouse, you called me a hippie. You thought I was like your mother."

"Only at first. Not anymore." He took one of the cookies off the plate. "For one thing, my mother never baked cookies."

"But she did have a considerable lack of appreciation for time, apparently. We have that in common."

He munched contentedly on the cookie, then said, "There's a big difference. My mother lived for today. You don't."

"I don't?"

"Your business wouldn't have been so successful if you had just drifted along. You and Melvin have deadlines and you meet them. That isn't how an irresponsible person operates."

"Darn. I've lost my amateur rating."

He brushed the crumbs off his hands, sweeping away her attempt to joke about herself. "Yup. You aren't as flaky as you try to make people think you are. Whether you like it or not, Whitney Grant, you happen to be a dependable adult. Sorry about that, but there you are."

Whitney carried her half-empty mug over to the sink and tossed the remaining hot chocolate down the drain. Taking her time, she rinsed out the cup and dried it with a paper towel. She didn't realize Stone had moved until she turned around and found him standing beside her.

"I think you're seeing only what you want to see, Stone," she said quietly.

"My eyesight is just fine."

"You're missing the point."

"No, I don't think I am, but you are." Lifting his hand, he let his fingers trail over the soft skin along her throat. "Why? Are you afraid?"

"What would I be afraid of?" she asked warily.

The back of his knuckles brushed the finely sculptured line of her jaw. "I hope it's not me you're afraid of. I'm relatively harmless."

That was the most hilarious remark she had ever heard, but she didn't feel like laughing. "So is a shark unless he's hungry."

He chuckled softly. "Then I guess I'm not so harmless after all because I'm very hungry."

Swallowing with difficulty, Whitney stared at him. His hunger was in his eyes and in his touch. His hands were warm and gentle cupping her face. He lowered his head, and she didn't turn away. Her eyes closed slowly and a soft sigh passed through her lips.

As his mouth claimed hers, she realized he wasn't just hungry. He was starving. It was impossible to resist the insistence of his kiss or his arms as he pulled her closer to his body.

Desire was like a writhing, greedy thing, coiling around them and pulling them into a maelstrom of need.

Without conscious thought, Whitney raised her arms to encircle his neck, her hands seeking the heat and strength of his shoulders and back. Under her palms, she felt his muscles clench and she marveled that her touch could affect him so strongly.

Stone's hands ran over the gentle curves of her shoulder, her spine, and her hips, and his imagination ran rampant as he thought of the body underneath her robe.

The pressure of his body against hers forced her back against the counter. His thigh slipped between her legs as his tongue surged between her lips. The combined assault weakened her knees and her resistance.

A soft feminine sound brushed against his mouth when he raised his head slightly, and he felt a savage satisfaction run through him. She wanted him as badly as he wanted her!

Moving his hands down her back, he found the belt around her waist. He followed it to the knot in front and his fingers began to loosen it. "Whitney," he murmured against her throat. "You make me ache down to my toes."

As his hands parted her robe, she gasped. "Stone, this is crazy."

"That's how you make me feel. Crazy."

His hands slipped under the robe, sliding over her waist and her hips, leaving a searing trail. Catching her mouth desperately with his, Stone felt a shattering exultation and a raw need stronger than anything he had ever experienced in his life. Even in his wildest dreams, she had never felt this good. *Nothing* had ever felt this good.

He cupped her breasts, his thumbs stroking, enticing, and tantalizing the hard tips. He raised his head enough to look down at her as he continued to caress her warm, satiny flesh. He watched in fascination as she slowly opened her eyes. They were dazed and dreamy. When her hands circled his neck to draw his head back down, he could have shouted in triumph. Even though she had said she didn't want to get involved with him, she couldn't resist the magic conjured up between them any more than he could.

The desire to possess her fully was strong. His gentleness ceased suddenly and he took her mouth with a desperate need to conquer the demons whirling inside him. What was it about her that drove him to the edge of sanity? Made him forget the vows he had made never to need anyone but himself, he wondered frantically as he ground his hips against hers.

Pulling his mouth away from hers, he groaned against her throat. "Tell me to go, Whitney."

"I . . . can't."

"Then tell me to stay."

"No. Not when you're angry."

He froze. She was right, he realized sickeningly. Beneath the desire was a simmering anger. Anger with himself, but he had directed it at her without knowing it. He wanted her, yet he didn't want to need her. Not emotionally. Physically his body was taut and aching and ready to make love to her, but something held him back. Making love with Whitney Grant wouldn't be just having sex, and he wasn't ready to admit what else it would be.

Reluctantly but firmly, he let his hands slide away from her tempting flesh. He closed her robe and gazed down at her, a myriad of emotions churning through him.

Whitney took a deep, steadying breath and tied the sash of her robe with trembling hands. She had learned a valuable lesson tonight. The man who had told her she was as responsive as one of her mechanical figures had been dead wrong. If she was any more responsive, she would go up in flames.

"I may never say it," she murmured, referring to his earlier request to ask him to stay.

He understood and took a deep breath. She was saying she might never go to bed with him. "Why?" he asked quietly.

"You may be attracted to me, Stone, but for some reason I make you angry. I could feel it when you kissed me."

He adjusted the collar of her robe to stand up around her throat, keeping the material between his hands and her skin. "It's not you, Whitney." Sighing, he raked his fingers through his hair. "I'm not sure what it is."

Needing to touch her one more time, he let his finger gently trace the shadows under her eyes. "I'll be back tomorrow to pick you up and take you to the wedding."

"You don't have to. I can drive myself."

"You'll go with me." It wasn't a request. It was an order.

He put his arm around her shoulders and started toward the door. When they reached the chair the rabbit was on, he picked up his jacket and patted the rabbit on the head. "Take care of her, pal."

At the door, Stone released her and drew on his jacket. He opened the door and looked back at her. Her fingers were clinging to the ends of her sash as though they were a lifeline. His hand tightened on the doorknob.

Regret and desire darkened his eyes and deepened his voice. "Good night, Whitney."

Her reply was hardly audible. "Good night."

As soon as her door shut behind Stone, Whitney walked slowly over to the rabbit. Picking it up, she hugged the stuffed animal briefly to her chest. The rabbit was a poor substitute and no comfort at all. She was about to put him back down when a dark object in the chair caught her eye.

She set the rabbit on the floor and picked up Stone's appointment book. It must have fallen out of his jacket, she thought as she stroked the soft leather. She hesitated for a split second, then opened it.

Five

The church pews were filled with friends and family of the bride and groom. The scent of the lavish floral arrangements blended with the subtle fragrance of the candles burning on the altar and in the elaborate candelabras on either side of the wedding party.

Standing several paces away from Sylvia, Whitney held the bride's bouquet and tried to keep her mind on the vows being exchanged. As she had been instructed during the rehearsal, she was turned partway toward the bride and groom, facing the best man. Her gaze and her attention kept wandering to Stone, who was standing straight and solemn on the other side of David.

He looked remote and unapproachable, as distant as he had been during the drive to the church. With his blond hair and black tuxedo, he was a marked contrast to the groom's dark hair and white tuxedo, which was exactly why Sylvia had chosen the combination.

Sylvia had also been responsible, too, for choosing the ankle-length dress in a shade of peach that Whitney wore. It was not her favorite color, and Whitney felt like a diminuitive sherbet confection, even though Sylvia had assured her the soft pastel complemented her hair and skin. The neckline was low and off her shoulders, the rest of the dress fitting to her knees, where the fabric flared out gently.

Stone was watching her, his expression as formal as his attire. She wished she knew what he was thinking. He might have been standing on a street corner waiting for a light to change for all the animation in his features. There was no sign of the passionate man who had taken her in his arms in her kitchen.

Looking away, she felt the raw ache inside that hadn't gone away since he had closed the door behind him last night. For hours she had sat on her couch with the lights off, holding his appointment book as she stared at the shadowy world outside her window. She had gone over every word, every touch between them, yet was still unable to come to terms with the unexpected anger he had shown her. Whatever had caused the anger, she didn't think it was her refusing to go to bed with him.

After learning about the way he had grown up, she was surprised he had come to her apartment. She would have expected him to stay as far away from her as he could. But he hadn't. Maybe that was part of the reason he'd been angry. He had come to her against his will, wanting her yet angry because he did. There was enough about her that was too similar to the irresponsible woman who had been his mother, and she couldn't fault him for feeling wary.

His inconsistent reactions to her were driving her crazy, though. First he didn't want to be involved, then he said he had to continue seeing her. He arranged to have her car fixed and last night became angry because he wanted her. The blasted man didn't know what in hell he wanted and she wasn't about to ride the seesaw of his emotions.

Last night she had mentally said good-bye to him. Emotionally would take a little longer, but she would do it. Life was full of choices and she had made hers. She had made compromises with her life in the past, but going to bed with a man who only wanted her body wasn't going to be one of them.

Because she was maid of honor, Whitney had to stand in the receiving line and later pose for pictures. The demanding photographer seemed to have an endless supply of film and poses for a wedding party. She obediently moved wherever he instructed, her smile frozen in place, especially when he paired her with the best man. Stone stood resolutely at her side while the camera was pointed at them.

The photographer gestured for her to move, and she shifted over several inches and inadvertently bumped into Stone's arm. She saw him jerk his hand away as though he couldn't stand touching her. His violent rejection hurt, but she refused to let him or anyone else see the pain.

At last they were all dismissed by the photographer and were able to go to the reception. She would have loved to call a taxi and go home to lick the wounds caused by her tight shoes and being near Stone. The only thing stopping her was the fact that Sylvia would be hurt if she left, so she went along to the reception hall with Stone as her escort. He apparently still considered it his duty to accompany her.

During the next several hours, Whitney endured enough polite conversation to last her for the next decade. Her early training as the daughter of a high-ranking naval officer provided her with the ability to mingle with people, saying just the right thing, dodging personal questions with ease.

The most frequent question was when it was going to be her turn to walk down the aisle. It was not her favorite question.

Once the band started playing, she was whisked out onto the floor by various men, members of Sylvia's and David's families, their friends, and complete strangers. She danced with tall men, old men, short men, and young men, until she felt as though her high heels were welded to her feet. As soon as she walked off the floor with one man, she was approached by another. Her shoes might hold out but she wasn't so sure about her toes. Sylvia's father might be a good banker, but he was in no danger of giving Arthur Murray any competition. He was the first of her partners to step on her toes, but he certainly wasn't the last.

Leaning a shoulder on one of the columns in the hall, Stone followed Whitney's progress on and off the dance floor. When she was first led out by Mr. Bascomb, it didn't bother him. When she continued to be held by one man after the other, however, he discovered something new about himself. He was jealous as hell and irrationally wanted to punch out every man she danced with. Along with all her college degrees, she must have taken a course in how to drive him crazy in three easy lessons, he thought grimly as he saw her exchange partners once again.

For a man who prided himself on being consistent, he was fast becoming a dithering idiot. One minute he was telling her he didn't think they should get involved with each other, and the next he was trying to push her into bed.

His eyes narrowed as he saw Mark Willis cut in on Whitney and her partner as the music changed to a throbbing rumba. Holding her tightly against him, Mark guided Whitney in a provocative dance step that had Stone gritting his teeth. Maybe if her partner had been anyone else but Mark Willis, he would have let it go. But Mark was the type of man who notched his bedpost with his many conquests, bragging about them in colorful detail.

When Mark placed his hand on Whitney's hip and began to move against her in an undulating rhythm in time to the heavy drum beat, Stone clenched his teeth so hard his jaw ached.

He pushed away from the column and nudged his way through the other couples on the dance floor. He tapped Mark on the shoulder. "I'm cutting in."

Mark looked like he was about to debate the issue but then he saw that at the moment Stone's expression reflected his name. Shrugging, he relinquished his hold on Whitney and went off to find another partner.

The band finished the seductive rumba melody and changed to a slow song as Stone pulled Whitney into his arms. Her body was stiff and rigid as his arm encircled her waist. He gazed down at her, but she wouldn't meet his eyes.

Whitney could feel the imprint of Stone's pleated cumberbund through her dress as his hand at her back pressed her against his hard body. With her hand on his shoulder, she was aware of the corded muscles underneath his tuxedo jacket. Steeling herself against the impact on her senses as her body molded to his, she refused to look at him, afraid of giving away more of her feelings than she had in the past.

A muscle clenched in his jaw, and when he spoke his voice was raw with frustration. "Is there some kind of quota for dancing with the most men? If there is, you should be more selective about who you dance with."

Considering she was dancing with him at the moment, she thought that was a rather strange comment to make. "At functions like this, it's polite to dance with everyone who asks."

"I didn't ask and you're dancing with me."

Smiling tightly, she qualified her statement. "It's polite to dance with whoever asks or cuts in."

"From now on don't be so polite."

She raised her eyes from his shirt front. "That sounds vaguely like an order."

"Probably because it was." He could feel her spine stiffen under his palm and added, "It doesn't matter anyway, since you won't be dancing with anyone else but me."

"Really?" she asked politely, her heart thudding heavily as she met his intense gaze. "Why is that?"

For a long moment, he simply looked at her. His green eyes were unusually dark. "Because I'll deck the next guy who touches you."

He spoke so casually, it took Whitney a moment to realize what he had said. It took her another few seconds to stop staring at him as though he had just lost his tiny mind. Finally, she asked, "Did you take one of your Dr. Jekyll, Mr. Hyde pills again today?"

Stone couldn't stop his smile, but didn't respond other than to pull her closer. He couldn't blame her for thinking he was two different men.

Seeing his smile, a tide of white fury washed over

her. Damn him, he was laughing at her! She jerked her right hand out of his and slid her other hand down to his chest, trying to push herself away from him. He wouldn't release her.

"Let me go, Stone," she said through tight lips.

He covered her hand on his chest, refusing to free her. "No."

"I can't take any more of this from you. You can't play these game with me."

"I'm not playing any games with you, Whitney."

She gave up any pretense of dancing with him. "What would you call it then? You seem to be having some kind of contest to see how many different ways you can treat me. Last night you wanted to make love to me, yet a little while ago when we were posing for the photographer, you couldn't bear to touch me. I want off this runaway roller coaster. I'm not enjoying the ride. I don't know what you want from me, Stone, and I don't think you know either."

He pressed his hand against her back, bringing her body to his. "I know what I want. I'm just not sure I should have it."

His words hurt. She tried again to break away from his grip, but without success. "Then I would just as soon sit this one out, thank you," she said hoarsely past the tightness in her throat. She wasn't referring to the dance but to the relationship. "Let me go."

"That's the problem. I can't." Moving again in time to the music, he forced her to dance with him, his hand keeping hers against his chest. Taking a deep breath, he continued, "I know you deserve an explanation and I'll try to give you one, but not here. Not now. After this is over."

Short of making a scene on the dance floor, she had

no option but to stay. His thighs rubbed against hers, sending waves of sweet agony through her. She stopped resisting him. "It looks like I don't have any choice."

"Not about who you'll dance with, but the choice will be up to you later after we talk."

As the evening wore on, Whitney saw that Stone had meant what he said. No other man danced with her or even came close to her, mainly because Stone had a possessive hand or arm on her at all times. The only time she was allowed to go anywhere alone was when she excused herself to go to the ladies' room.

As she washed her hands she tried to make sense out of Stone's behavior. She had no idea what he was going to say to her . . . or whether she wanted to hear it.

Her body fought a battle with her mind. For years she had lived in a vacuum of her own making. There had been no affairs, no involvements with men lasting longer than two or three dates, none of them ending in her bedroom. She had never even been tempted. She had never before experienced the feelings Stone created just by being near her. For the first time in her life, she wanted a man physically. There were a million and one reasons why it scared her, but the main one was that she was afraid of being devastated when it turned out a physical relationship was all he wanted from her.

An hour later the newly married couple left in a flurry of confetti and well-wishers waving them off. Brushing colorful bits of paper out of her hair, Whitney felt Stone's hand lightly skim over her shoulders and back. Her fingers stilled and she lowered her arm.

Slowly turning her head, she looked up and caught the sensual warmth glowing in his eyes.

"If you're ready to go, I'll take you home." His voice was quietly serious.

She could tell him she wasn't ready but that would only be postponing the inevitable and would accomplish nothing. He was ready to talk to her, to give her an explanation of his strange behavior. But was she ready to hear it? she wondered wearily.

She put her hand on his arm for balance. "Just a minute," she murmured, and proceeded to remove her shoes. She plucked her housekey from inside her right shoe. "Is there a pocket in that tuxedo?"

"Yes," he answered carefully. "Why?"

"This dress doesn't have any." She held out the key. "Will you hold this for me until I get home?"

He took the key and slipped it into a pocket. "Don't you like purses?"

"I didn't have one to match this dress." She sighed blissfully and wiggled her toes. "I couldn't have taken another step in these shoes. Forget bamboo strips under fingernails. Tight shoes are worse torture."

He couldn't prevent the smile that curved his mouth as he took her arm and started toward his car. She was so delightfully natural without any pretense or phoniness. It was one of her many charms.

"Why did you buy them if they are uncomfortable?"

"There aren't a lot of selections in my size. I usually have to get shoes in the children's department. When we lived in Japan, I was in shoe heaven. It's the land of little feet."

Thinking of the decorations on the wall of her home, he added, "And the land of Oriental fans. Is that where you started to collect them?"

"No. It was before our tour in Japan. When my father was stationed in Hawaii, a diplomat from Japan gave my mother and me each a silk fan as a gift. It sort of started there and grew."

He opened the door for her. "Japan and Hawaii. You've been around."

"Join the navy and see the world doesn't apply just to the sailors."

After she was seated, Stone went to the front of the car and slid in behind the wheel. Before starting the car, he removed his black tie and several studs from his shirt.

He saw she was watching him and smiled faintly. "Tight collars are as uncomfortable as tight shoes."

"What we don't do out of friendship." Like escorting the maid of honor to a wedding, she thought. Well, the wedding was over and so was the reason for Stone to continue seeing her. Was that what he wanted to talk about?

"I didn't realize what a big production a wedding was," he said with feeling. "At least this one was. They could use Sylvia in Hollywood as a director of spectaculars."

"She wanted her wedding to be perfect since it's the only one she plans to have."

"I suppose women look at weddings differently from men. David's relieved it's all over. He only went through it because it's what Sylvia wanted."

"So when you get married, you don't plan on a big production?" she asked, and added lightly. "I bet Sylvia would be willing to help with the arrangements."

"Since I don't plan on getting married, I won't need Sylvia's help," he said bluntly. He saw her stiffen at the harshness in his voice. Purposely softening his tone, he asked, "How about you? Daddy Admiral could give you a wedding with crossed swords you and the groom could parade under."

"Daddy Admiral would get the swords out only if I married a military man, which isn't going to happen."

"Don't you like military men? I thought women liked men in uniform."

She preferred men in tuxedos at the moment, but she wasn't about to say so. "Not enough to marry one, or a civilian man either. Like you, I'm not into weddings." Not especially enjoying the topic of conversation, she changed it and she looked pointedly at the car keys in his hand. "Are we waiting for anything in particular?"

He turned the key in the ignition. "Would you like to get something to eat? You didn't have much at the buffet."

She would rather be on her own turf when he said what he had to say. "I would just as soon get out of these clothes." She closed her eyes as she realized what she had said. For a perfectly innocent statement, it could be taken any number of ways.

Stone took it at face value. "Are there any chocolate chip cookies left?"

"Yes," she replied cautiously, wondering what cookies had to do with anything. "Why?"

"I'll munch on a couple of cookies and make a pot of coffee while you change into your grungy tennis shoes."

Whitney gazed out the side window. She wasn't sure she wanted their last time together to be prolonged. It would be easier if he dropped her off at her door and simply drove away. Then she remembered his appointment book. She had meant to give it back to him when he picked her up, but she had been running late and was still getting dressed when he rang her doorbell. In the rush to get to the church, she had forgotten all about it.

Stone took her silence as consent. The closest parking spot he could find was about half a block away and they received a few stares from people as they walked to her apartment building. Even in San Francisco, the sight of a barefooted woman in a formal dress carrying her shoes and walking beside a man wearing a tuxedo without a tie at three in the afternoon was a curiosity.

Since he had her key, Stone unlocked the door and opened it, standing to one side to allow her to go in first. He followed and shut the door behind him.

"You go ahead and change. I know where you keep the cookies."

"Your appointment book is on the counter. It dropped out of your jacket pocket last night. I'll only be a minute."

Stone stared after her as she closed the door of her bedroom. He automatically reached for his breast pocket, forgetting for a moment he wore a tuxedo instead of a suit. Dropping his hand, he walked toward the bar and picked up his appointment book. He hadn't even missed it. He hardly made a move without it and he hadn't noticed it was gone!

He tossed the book back onto the bar in disgust, then went into the kitchen to make coffee and get the cookies. He munched on a cookie as he stared out of the living room window at the spectacular view of San Francisco, wondering what in hell he was doing here. If he didn't think Whitney deserved an explanation about his bizarre behavior toward her, he would simply leave. He had never considered he had cowardly tendencies, but right now, he had a yellow streak down his back a mile wide. His mouth twisted into a grimace. After he told her why he had been acting like a royal jackass, she might show him the door anyway.

Was he making a mistake in attempting to explain himself to her? he wondered for about the tenth time.

He still didn't have the answer when she left her bedroom wearing a pair of faded jeans and a navy blue T-shirt with U.S. NAVY printed on the front in bold gold letters. Her tiny feet were bare, adding to the impression of a casually-dressed teenager. His heated gaze roamed over her slender hips and breasts. They dispelled any thoughts of her as a child.

He followed her into the kitchen, where she took down two mugs from a cabinet. Her hand accidentally hit the spoon he had used to measure the coffee grounds and it fell on the floor. She bent down to pick it up, and his gaze was immediately riveted to her hips and thighs. His blood ran hot, searing his veins with a wildfire of sensual need. His hands burned to stroke her tempting body. How in the hell was he going to be able to talk coherently when all he wanted to do was bury himself deep inside her?

Whitney could feel the air sizzle and crackle with the power of the attraction between them. Even though she recognized it, she didn't plan to encourage it. This would be the last time she would be with him and she was going to say good-bye with her pride intact. She cared for him more than was wise or sensible, but that was going to remain her secret, not to be shared with him or anyone else.

She poured the coffee and carried his over to him, but he didn't immediately take the mug from her. He was concentrating all his attention on her. Seeing the half-eaten cookie in his hand, she said casually, "I see you found the cookies."

"I'll share." He offered her the cookie, and since her hands were full, she simply leaned forward and took a bite out of it.

Coils of desire tightened his gut as she ran her tongue over her bottom lip to catch an errant crumb. He was dying by inches and she was calmly chewing on a cookie. When she raised her eyes, she smiled at him. He quickly finished off the cookie, his hands curling into fists as he tried to control the urge to give in to his own need, reflected in her eyes. Unclenching his hands, he took several paces away and removed the tuxedo jacket.

"Shall we sit down?" he suggested. "This may take awhile and we might as well be comfortable."

As Whitney walked into the living room, she wondered how long it could possibly take to say good-bye. She placed his coffee mug on the glass and mahogany table in front of the couch. Curling her feet under her, she sat down on the couch, leaning against the plump arm. She rested her mug of coffee on her knees as he tossed his jacket over the back of the same chair he had used as a coat rack last night. His cuff links were next. He dropped them onto the coffee table before turning back the cuffs of his shirt several turns.

For a man about to say so long, he was certainly taking his time getting to it, she thought. "Just how comfortable do you plan on getting?" she asked, a touch of irony in her voice. "If you go for your shoes next, I'm going to have something to say."

Stone gave her a thin smile. "You can relax. I didn't come here for a seduction."

"Silly me. I must have misinterpreted your taking off your clothes."

He sat down next to her, then reached for his mug of

coffee and settled back. "Not that I wouldn't rather be seducing you than talking."

"You could take the easy way out and just simply say good-bye, it's been nice to know you, and get it over with."

He looked startled. "Good-bye? Is that what you think this is all about?"

"The confetti's been thrown and Sylvia and David have left for their honeymoon. There's no need for the best man to escort the maid of honor anymore."

He shifted slightly until he was facing her, his knee near her hip, his arm draped over the back of the couch. "I don't need an excuse to keep seeing you, Whitney."

"I would like a reason why you would want to."

His mouth twisted humorlessly. "Yes, I imagine you do. I've given you a hard time and you deserve to know why."

Whitney waited, hardly breathing, unsure she was going to like what she was about to hear.

"Your experience may be different," he began, "but I don't know anyone who has a long-term relationship that is working out. Quite a while ago I decided to play the field. The longest I ever went with a woman was three, sometimes four dates. Less if she showed signs of becoming possessive or taking it for granted we were seriously involved."

Even though the occasions they had been together couldn't be classified as dates, Whitney thought, this was the fourth time they had seen each other.

"Four strikes and they're out?" she asked.

"Something like that." He raked his fingers through his hair, indicating a distracted, vaguely impatient emotion. "I wasn't about to go through the same things friends and business associates were going through. Divorces, tearful recriminations, alimony, custody battles, stepchildren." He paused, then added mockingly, "It seemed so messy."

"And you're a man who likes his life neat and tidy."

"That was the plan. A neat and tidy life on my terms."

For lack of anything else to say, Whitney murmured, "There could be worse plans."

He set his mug down and stood. He walked around the coffee table and turned to her, his hand on his hips. "Like all plans, sometimes they don't work out the way we want them to. This one started out as Sylvia's plan. She asked me to escort you to the wedding rehearsal and then to the wedding. It sounded relatively simple and straightforward. Then I met you and things got complicated. Occasionally I forgot the plan, like when I picked you up in Union Square and when I kissed you here last night."

Little pieces of the puzzle were falling into place. "You were following your plan the night of the wedding rehearsal when you told me we shouldn't get involved."

His gaze held hers as he answered honestly, "Yes. Then I deviated when I impulsively picked you up at Union Square and again when I came here last night."

Shadows darkened her blue eyes. "And remembered again when the photographer was taking photos after the wedding." Her voice was flat and emotionless.

A frown of puzzlement creased his brow. Seeing it, she explained, "I accidentally brushed against you when I was moving where the photographer wanted me to stand, and you reacted as if you had touched a rather nasty poisonous toad."

Hearing the pain in her voice, though she was trying to disguise it by adopting a light tone, he moved toward her, kneeling on one knee in front of her. He took her mug from her and set it aside before taking her hands in his. "Whitney, I jerked away from you because touching you, even innocently as that was, causes certain unmistakable reactions that even an expensive tuxedo can't hide."

A soft blush tinted her cheeks as his meaning became clear to her. "Oh," she murmured.

His fingers tightened around hers, his thumbs stroking the back of her hands. "Like now. In the beginning the way I responded to you scared the hell out of me. Every time I was around you, touched you, or kissed you, I burned with wanting you. Your smile ignited my bloodstream and touching you was like stroking satin fire. It took awhile for me to come to terms with the fact that those feelings wouldn't disappear. At least not right away."

Her mind repeated his last comment. "At least not right away." Whether he realized it or not, he was putting a time limit on his interest, even if it was ambiguous.

"So what are you trying to say?" she asked. "That we go on or stop right here?"

"I don't honestly know if I would be any good in a long-term relationship, Whitney. Maybe I'm not cut out for a close involvement with a woman, but for the first time in my life I would like to try."

The thudding of her heart seemed almost deafening to her. "What kind of relationship do you have in mind? Acquaintances, friends, lovers?"

His smile was crooked. "Hell, I don't know, Whitney. I told you. I'm new at this. I haven't the faintest idea how a relationship works."

"I imagine it's a lot like marriage or becoming a

parent. You take it a day at a time. You learn as you go along. You make mistakes. You compromise. You share the good times and the bad."

Without letting go of her hands, he straightened until he was standing in front of her. With a gentle but persistent tug on her hands, he drew her off the couch. "I've told you what I want. Now I need to hear what you want."

He didn't ask for much. She saw the tension in his eyes and around his mouth, felt it in his hands. It seemed to matter what her answer might be.

"Right now I'd like a hug," she said softly.

Surprise widened his eyes, then he smiled. "That's easy enough."

He slid his arms around her waist and across her back. The hug contained comfort and pleasure and for the moment was without passion. They clung together, absorbing the shared warmth and the companionship, their hearts beating normally and in rhythm.

But gradually the embrace changed. Stone's hands began to glide over her back without any motive other than the pure luxury of caressing her. Whitney moved closer, seeking his heat. Desire grew between them. Their pulses accelerated and the banked embers of attraction were in danger of becoming a raging fire.

Taking a ragged breath, Stone loosened his hold and stepped back. "I promised myself I would control myself with you," he muttered, sounding thoroughly disgusted with himself. "I didn't realize how difficult that promise was going to be to keep."

"What if I said I don't want you to keep that promise?" she asked, surprising herself as well as him.

He dragged his gaze back to hers, the hunger inside him sparking green flames in his eyes. An unsteady hand lifted toward her, then he lowered it to his side.

America's most popular, most compelling romance novels...

Here, at last...love stories that really involve you! Fresh, finely crafted novels with story lines so believable you'll feel you're actually living them! Characters you can relate to...exciting places to visit...unexpected plot twists...all in all, exciting romances that satisfy your mind and delight your heart.

After a brief struggle with himself, he growled, "Don't tempt me right now, Whitney. I'm hanging on by a mere thread."

She watched as he picked up their coffee mugs and walked into the kitchen. He set them on the bar and they were in the same positions as they had been the previous night, except they had changed places. She sat down on a stool and he leaned back against the kitchen counter.

"Your . . . controlling yourself," she said, a slight tremor in her voice. "Is this another case of wanting things neat and tidy?"

"People go to bed with each other all the time, Whitney. For a variety of reasons. Most of them selfish. Without any meaning other than minutes of gratification."

He was looking at her but Whitney felt he wasn't really seeing her. Shadows haunted his eyes. Her instincts told her he was remembering another time, another place, another circumstance that wasn't particularly pleasant.

He went on. "Responsibility for conceiving a child doesn't enter into the act on either side. It's the sex that's important. Sometimes names aren't even exchanged, although money occasionally is. Sex is easy to get if that's what you want."

Whitney had a feeling he was talking about the things he had seen growing up in the Haight-Ashbury district when the area was a mecca for society dropouts who wanted to create their own rules and life-styles. Or perhaps he was talking about his mother. Of course, there was always the possibility he was talking about himself.

He pushed away from the counter and approached the bar. "To me there's a difference between a one-night stand and a relationship. I would like to try having a relationship with you. Only you." He waited for a long tense moment, his eyes never leaving her face. "What do you think?"

Instead of answering his question directly, Whitney reached for his appointment book and drew it toward her. She picked up the pen from next to the telephone and flipped through the date book until she found the page for the following day. Without hesitation, she printed something on the page.

Trying to read upside down without much success, Stone gave it up and stepped around the bar to stand beside her. He looked over her shoulder. Under Sunday, she had printed: *Have picnic with Whitney Grant, Eleven A.M., Golden Gate Park. Bring wine.*

The coil of tension in his stomach began to loosen and a heavy weight eased off his shoulders. He hadn't realized it was there until he began to relax. He had his answer.

He took the pen from her, then reached around her from behind and turned the page to Monday. Holding the book open, with his free hand he wrote, *"Dinner with Whitney. Seven P.M. Order flowers to be sent to Whitney."*

His chest was warm and solid against her back as she took the pen out of his hand and scratched out the last part of his note. "I don't need flowers, Stone."

His arms crossed over in front of her, his forearms pressing against her breasts. Lowering his head, he spoke against the side of her neck. "I need to get them for you."

She rested her head back against his shoulder. "Are you sure this is what you want, Stone? We're too such different people. If we get involved, we might end up hating each other."

He raised his hands to her shoulders and turned her around to face him. Lifting her face with a finger under her chin, he said softly, "We're already involved, Whitney." He stroked the soft skin along her jaw. "And we're going to get a whole lot more involved."

His hands on her waist, he lifted her off the stool. He had to steel his resolve to leave now while he could. His promise was becoming almost impossible to keep. Her creamy skin and the slender lines of her body beckoned to be touched and her special scent clouded his judgment. He needed to get out of there while he still could.

He dropped his hands. "I'll see you tomorrow at eleven."

Her confusion was evident in her eyes as she looked up at him. "You're leaving?"

He nodded slowly.

She picked up his notebook and handed it to him. "You might need this."

He tucked the book into his cummerbund. "Will you be here or at the warehouse?"

There were a few things he was going to have to accept about her too, she thought. At the moment she planned to be here waiting for him, but she might get an urge to work on one of the projects at the warehouse in the meantime. "Try here first."

Gathering up his cuff links and coat, he headed toward the door, throwing the tuxedo jacket over his arm instead of putting it on. He opened the door, then paused to look back at her. Smiling faintly, he left.

A sound of disbelief, exasperation, and amusement came from Whitney's parted lips. Just like that and he was gone. The least they could have done was shake hands or something.

Disgruntled, she stared at the door. If this was his idea of a relationship, it left a lot to be desired.

She wasn't the daughter of Admiral Stewart "Gung Ho" Grant, Retired, for nothing. Tomorrow she was going to instruct Stone on a few pertinent details of what she expected from their relationship. If she had to make notes in his appointment book so he would set aside time for a proper good night, she would do it.

He might even get the hang of saying good morning.

Six

When Whitney opened the drapes covering the large window the following morning, the sun had cut through a light fog still hovering over the water. It was going to be a beautiful day for a picnic.

She quickly pulled on a blue jogging outfit and tied her running shoes. She tucked some money into a nylon pouch that fastened on her wrist with Velcro straps. After leaving her apartment, she dropped her key into the pouch and set off into the early morning air.

An hour later, she returned carrying a large bag of groceries. She put away the items that needed to be refrigerated, then went into the bathroom to take a shower.

By ten-thirty, the old wicker picnic basket she had found in a second-hand store was packed and ready. Each fitted tin container was full of food she had picked up at a local delicatessen. In one corner was a small sack of chocolate chip cookies. The linen napkins, bone-handled silverware, the crystal glasses, and small china plates were all tucked into their proper places and secured by straps. A red plaid blanket was neatly folded on the bar next to the basket.

Whitney chose white clam-digger pants and a long-sleeved white knit top with narrow navy strips, pushing the sleeves up her forearms. Instead of the comfortable old sneakers Stone teased her about, she dug out a pair of relatively new tennis shoes from the bottom of her closet and put them on. She also took out a short bomber jacket in case the weather turned cool.

Her doorbell rang at exactly eleven o'clock. When she opened the door, her welcoming smile wavered a little as she saw how well Stone's jeans molded to his slim hips and long legs, and how his hunter green cotton sweater worn over a white shirt complemented his eyes. Those same eyes surveyed her from head to toe, golden lights flickering in their depths as he approved of what he saw.

The man could wear anything from a formal tuxedo to casual jeans and still take her breath away, she thought, which was probably why her voice sounded weak when she invited him to come in.

He lifted his hand toward her and she automatically took it, clasping her fingers around his. He leaned down and kissed her lightly.

"Hi."

She responded with a frail "Hi."

Still holding her hand, he stepped into the foyer. "I was listening to the weather forecast on the radio as I was driving over here. There's a possibility of rain later, but I'm willing to chance a picnic if you are."

She looked at the sunny view out her window. The sky was light blue without a sign of a rain cloud. Of course, that could all change, but for now it was a lovely day.

Turning her attention back to Stone, she smiled. "I'm not afraid of a little rain." She tugged gently at his hand and led him over to the bar. "If you'll carry the basket, I'll take the blanket and my jacket."

Stone lifted the basket by its handle and made an exaggerated face as though it weighed a ton. "Did you happen to slip in a few of your tools when you were packing this?"

She picked up the blanket and slung her jacket over her arm. "Come on, Superman. You'll be singing a different tune when you see all I've got in there. You won't need to eat for a week."

"I believe it." He nodded toward the blanket in her arms. "Give me that. I'll carry it so you can lock your door."

He stood beside her as she slipped the key in the lock and turned it. She was about to drop the key in the pocket of her clam-diggers when he said, "Put it in my pocket. If you start turning cartwheels or something, you may lose it."

She grinned up at him. "I don't plan on turning cartwheels. I plan on eating."

"Put it in my pocket anyway."

She studied him carefully. Since his hands were full, he couldn't very well put the key in his pocket. She would have to do it herself. Unless it was her imagination, there was a challenge in his eyes. She decided to take him up on it.

His jeans were incredibly snug. She had to flatten her hand to run her fingers and palm over his hip in order to get the key securely in his pocket. The coarse material of his jeans rasped against her skin, but she wasn't aware of it. His simple request had become an incredibly intimate experience. The heat from his body radiated up her arm and into her stomach as she slowly withdrew her hand.

She raised her eyes to meet his. "Well, that was certainly more interesting than putting the key in my shoe," she said huskily.

Stone shifted. His jeans had suddenly become binding and uncomfortable. "I may throw away all your purses and shoes from now on."

"I may let you."

His eyes slammed into hers. Desire rippled in the air around them like a living, breathing thing. It was acknowledged in the way their gazes locked and their breathing accelerated. The acceptance was there but so was caution.

Stone tucked the folded blanket under his arm, freeing a hand in order to hold it out to her. Slowly, she lifted her hand and clasped his, the gesture one of willingness to go on to face whatever was ahead.

As they walked to his car Stone held her hand, content for now to have her at his side without needing anything more. Being with Whitney filled a spot inside him he never knew was empty until he had met her. She made him happy. It was that simple and that profound. There was a wellspring of joy inside her that bubbled out to wash over those around her, and he was becoming dependent on that feeling, needing it to be complete.

Even though the undercurrent of sexual attraction remained with them, they merely accepted it as a constant companion, allowing it to exist without having to acknowledge it. They enjoyed the lunch Whitney had packed, consuming almost everything in the basket along with the bottle of white wine Stone had provided.

Whitney was pleased when Stone exclaimed enthusiastically about the china dishes, the bone-handled silverware, the crystal glasses. He was sprawled out on his side, propped up on one elbow, and his eyes held a teasing glint. "I can see you believe in doing things with style, Whitney. I would love to see how you serve a TV dinner."

She grimaced. "Plastic food deserves plastic dishes, not china."

He raised his goblet to make a toast. "To my first picnic."

She automatically clinked her glass with his, the delicate chime ringing for a few seconds, even as she stared at him in astonishment. "You've never been on a picnic before?"

He sipped the wine. "Not that I can remember. Unless you count eating fast-food hamburgers while sitting beside my mother's jewelry stand. Or wolfing down a hot dog on the way to class at Berkeley." Amusement flickered in his eyes and curved his mouth. "Apparently you're an old hand at them."

"I love picnics. There's something gloriously casual in sitting on the ground or at a picnic table eating with your fingers, swatting away flies and bees, and dodging ants. Dining at home was always gruesomely ritualistic. Even if there were no guests, my father insisted on meals at a certain time with the proper dress and decorum. He's the only person I know who could make breakfast a formal meal. I remember the first time I ever stayed overnight with a girlfriend. Her mother was wearing a bathrobe while she cooked breakfast, and she served it on the kitchen table. It was a revelation. My mother and I were required to be dressed for the day before sitting down to eat at the dining room table."

Stone couldn't take his gaze off her expressive face. Enthusiasm glittered in her eyes when she talked about picnics, then faded when she spoke of the meals she had suffered through while growing up. He was reminded of a butterfly who had been confined to a hothouse and now was free.

"When did you first discover picnics?" he asked.

"It wasn't a picnic exactly. Sylvia had a slumber party out in their backyard, sleeping in tents. I think Mrs. Bascomb didn't want all us grubby girls messing up her pristine kitchen, so she suggested we cook our own breakfast on their barbecue. We burnt the sausages, fried the eggs to a crisp, and ended up with black toast." Her sigh was pure rapture. "It was wonderful."

He laughed. "It sounds like it."

"I like breakfast picnics the best. Especially at sunrise. Even if it's only a sweet roll and a cup of coffee. It's a terrific way to start the day."

Animation lit up her eyes, and Stone thought he would rather start the day by seeing her head on the pillow next to his. It would be like watching the sun rise to have her blue eyes open to meet his. "Now that I'm getting the hang of this picnic stuff," he said, "perhaps we could try a breakfast picnic next."

"What do you like to eat for breakfast?"

"Anything but graham crackers," he murmured dryly as he reached for a potato chip.

"Graham crackers aren't my idea of breakfast food."

"They weren't mine either but they're what I ate practically every morning. Usually broken up into a bowl of milk. If I was in a hurry, I would grab a couple of squares and eat them on the way to school."

The more she heard about his childhood, the more

she realized what he had overcome in order to be the person he was today. Knowing the last thing he wanted was pity, she said lightly, "I promise. No graham crackers."

"Then I'm all for a breakfast picnic. What is your favorite breakfast?"

"Anything but grapefruit, a soft-boiled egg, and a piece of toast." She grinned. "That's what I had every morning without fail when I lived at home. I was as sick of the same old thing as you were of graham crackers."

"And you're a lady who likes variety."

She picked up a peach. "When you've had a steady diet of steak, it's a welcome treat to sample a juicy hamburger once in a while. It's the same as dressing up in your finest clothes, like the tuxedo you wore yesterday. It would get pretty boring to have to wear it all the time." She stopped and considered for a moment. "Of course, it can work the other way too. After wearing my jeans and coveralls for weeks at a time, it's a nice change for me to put on something pretty and feminine."

Glints of mischief flickered in his eyes. "Afraid of getting into a rut, Whitney? That's the last thing you have to worry about."

"I suppose not." She bit into the peach, and sighed her delight with the succulent taste. A strange sound came from Stone, and she glanced at him. Her eyes widened when she saw his expression. He was staring at her mouth as though he were starving and she had the last bite of food. Her tongue automatically darted out to catch the juice on her bottom lip, and he made that sound again.

Before she could guess what he was going to do, he

swiftly sat up and framed her face with his hands. Then he licked the remaining drops of peach juice from her lips.

"Delicious," he murmured against her mouth. "You taste like everything delicious in this world."

Once the fruity taste was gone, he feasted on her mouth, gently savoring her. As he caressed and nibbled her bottom lip, she made a sound similar to the one he had made a few moments ago. The half-eaten peach fell from her numb fingers to the grass, forgotten as a different hunger replaced the desire for food.

Warm, strong fingers gripped her shoulders, and he pulled her onto his lap. "I think I could become addicted to picnics if they always taste this good," he said huskily as his teeth nipped and teased her lips.

She lifted her arms to encircle his neck as he deepened the quest of her mouth. A soft, yearning moan vibrated between them, neither one aware of who it came from and not really caring. Heedless of the occasional jogger running past them or the bicycle riders pedaling by, Stone took her mouth and gave her pleasure in return.

Her fingers dug into his back as his tongue plunged into her mouth. His hand moved down to knead her breast through the thin material of her top, and she arched her back in response, bringing her softness more fully into his hand. Her hips shifted restlessly across his thighs.

"Stone." She moaned again, not sure what she wanted to say, just needing to speak his name.

As though she had said something, he muttered, "I know."

Suddenly his hand left her breast. He gripped her arms and set her back onto the blanket next to him.

Bringing his knees up and resting his arms on them, he bowed his head. His breathing was raw and painful as he gasped to fill his lungs.

It took a few seconds for Whitney to come out of the fog of arousal, and she inhaled deeply. The sun was disappearing behind dark clouds, but that wasn't why she felt chilled. She had been plunged into the fiery furnace of Stone's desire, enflamed by her own needs, and then the passion had been abruptly doused, leaving her feeling stranded and aching.

She lifted her hand to touch him, but he must have sensed what she was about to do. His voice was muffled yet clear enough for her to hear. "Don't. Just give me a minute."

She let her hand drop to her side. Gradual awareness of their surroundings gave her the answer to why he had stopped so abruptly. Unlike her, Stone had realized where they were and had put an end to the blaze of desire before it raged out of control.

It was a little frightening to discover she could forget everything except how good it felt to be in his arms. She studied his bent head, watching how the wind tousled his hair and longing to let her fingers imitate that caressing motion. He looked oddly defenseless and vulnerable as he tried to regain control of his rioting emotions. She wished she had the right to put her arms around him to comfort him.

Or the right to love him.

Pain squeezed her heart, and she looked away. Love wasn't what he wanted from her. That hurt, because he had had so little love in his life and she had so much love to give him. And she did love him. For all the good it did.

The weather was matching her mood. The sun was

gone completely now and the day was gloomy. The wind had become stronger and cooler as it blew in from the ocean, bringing dark, threatening clouds with it. Several drops of rain trickled down, a hint of what the weather forecaster had predicted.

"Stone?"

"I know." He raised his head and gazed at her. "It looks like Mother Nature has decided to try her own way to cool me off."

A strong gust of wind whipped an edge of the blanket up off the ground and knocked over a glass of wine. Whitney quickly began gathering up the plates and containers of food.

"I think Mother Nature is trying to tell us we're going to get very wet if we don't move."

"Aside from the fact that I would benefit from a cold shower right now, I think we'd better hurry."

He helped her put everything back into the picnic basket, and as he closed the lid, the rain increased in intensity. He yanked up the blanket and tucked it under his arm, then grabbed the basket and Whitney's hand.

"Let's make a run for it."

The rain was coming down heavily by the time they reached the car. They were both soaked and Whitney hesitated to get in.

"I'll get the seat wet."

"So it gets wet. Get in."

Once he had joined her inside the car, he took out his handkerchief and handed it to her. "Is this part of picnics too?"

"Sometimes," she said, dabbing at the moisture on her face. She grinned suddenly. "Fun, huh?"

"It's a riot," he drawled. "What happens when you're still hungry and there's food left?"

She handed him back his handkerchief. "You eat the food. Just somewhere else. Why? Are you still hungry?"

The look he gave her spoke volumes. "That's a stupid question if you remember back to a few minutes ago. Hell, yes, I'm hungry."

"I meant for food."

"That too."

"We could have a picnic here in the car." He didn't seem too excited about that idea, so she offered another. "Or we could go back to my apartment and spread the blanket on the floor in the living room."

He started the engine. "Good idea but too far away."

The windshield wipers could barely keep up with the steady wash of water. Visibility was next to nothing as Whitney looked out the window. She hadn't the faintest idea where they were going, but for the moment she didn't care. Ever since she had met Stone, she had felt as though she were nearing the edge of a steep cliff. She kept stepping back to where it was safe instead of taking the plunge into unknown territory. It was time to take that step forward.

If he had been surprised to see where she lived, it was nothing to her reaction when she saw where he lived.

Since the rain was coming down in a steady blinding sheet, she wasn't able to see the front of the house clearly as he pulled into the driveway. The blurred view was of trees and shrubs and a two-story brick house. Stone pushed a button above his visor and the garage door began to rise. Once inside, Stone opened a door off the garage and stepped back for her to enter the house first. She walked into a brick-tiled entranceway, then up a step to the kitchen. She removed her wet shoes and looked around. Her first impression was of walnut cupboards, white marble counters, gleaming white appliances, and the same brick flooring.

"You'd better get out of those wet clothes," Stone said, coming up behind her. "I'll find you something to wear while your clothes dry."

She followed him down a long hallway to a large bedroom. While he rummaged around in a closet that took up an entire wall, she examined the furnishings. Light blue walls with dark woodwork complemented the dark furniture and dark blue bedspread. An Oriental carpet graced the hardwood floor, white with blue designs and a blue border.

Smiling, Stone watched her turn slowly as she looked around the room. Even with bedraggled hair and wet clothes, she was the most beautiful sight he had ever seen. His gaze lowered to the front of her knit shirt where her breasts were clearly outlined under the clinging damp fabric. His fingers tightened on the robe he had pulled from the closet. He had been in a state of semiarousal ever since he had picked her up at her apartment, and it hadn't been easy to recover from the brief episode of lovemaking in the park.

Now she was in his bedroom where he had pictured her numerous times.

When he saw her hug her arms to ward off the chill from her wet clothes, he said her name to get her attention. She looked at him and he tossed her the robe. "You can use the bathroom off the bedroom. I'll use the guest bath."

For a long moment, her eyes held his, then she smiled faintly. "Would you mind if I took a shower? I'm freezing."

His body became taut and hard as the thought of her standing naked under his shower sent flares of need through him. He shook his head and abruptly turned back to the closet to disguise his aroused state. He didn't turn around until he heard the door to the bathroom close behind her.

The sound of running water filtered through the door and he yanked clothes off their hangers before leaving the bedroom. A man could only take so much.

After an extremely uncomfortable cold shower, Stone dressed in a pair of faded jeans and pulled on a cream-colored sweater. Raking his fingers through his damp hair, he left the bathroom, hoping Whitney was out of the shower by now.

He stopped in the doorway of his bedroom and saw her sitting on his bed, her legs crossed Indian-style, his robe falling off her shoulders and draped over her lap. She was using the bedside phone, listening with a look of irritation on her face.

When she saw him in the doorway, she gestured to him to come in. He smiled. It was his bedroom to begin with. "Why can't you go?" she said into the phone. After a short pause, she gave an exasperated sigh and said, "All right. I'll go but under protest."

She hung up the phone and leaned back against the padded headboard. A frown marred her usually cheerful expression as she looked at Stone. The ticking of the clock on the table near the bed seemed obscenely loud to Stone as he watched her fold back the sleeves of his robe. For the first time since he'd met her, she appeared to be pouting, obviously sulking about something.

"What's wrong?"

"That rat Melvin ducked out of going to the opening of a gallery in Ghirardelli Square tonight. The contract calls for one of us to be there to make sure the display in the window works properly. He knows I don't want to go, but he said he needs to work on the darn dragon." Her expression suddenly changed and she smiled. Shifting her position, she knelt and held out her hand. "Sit down a minute. I have a proposition for you."

His voice was rough when he spoke. "I'm not one of your damn robots made of electrical wiring and metal, Whitney. If I join you on that bed, it won't be to talk." He saw the shock in her eyes and turned away. "Oh, hell," he muttered under his breath as he left the bedroom.

Stunned by his sudden flash of anger, Whitney didn't immediately move. Then she slipped off the bed and went after him.

Pausing in the wide arched doorway of the living room, she saw him standing in front of a window he had opened. The rain had dwindled to a mere shower and a light breeze ruffled his hair. He looked vital and elemental against the backdrop of the gray rain. And lonely.

Her bare feet made no sound as she entered the living room. It was a beautiful room, as totally unexpected as she had found his bedroom. The walls were a dark green. Dark walnut tables offset a cream sofa and the matching chairs, which were covered in a floral print of cream and green. An antique desk sat along one wall and a glass-fronted hutch displayed books and various porcelain figures. A cream Oriental rug covered a portion of the gleaming hardwood floor.

Without having to ask, she knew he was responsible for the furnishings in his house, not an anonymous decorator. Having never had a real home before, he had created one for himself full of the sorts of things that represented warmth and security to him.

The breeze coming through the open window was cool and damp as she walked toward him. She stopped several feet away. "Stone?"

He had known she was in the room even though she had made no sound until she said his name. Instead of answering, he shut the window. Then he turned around and simply looked at her.

"I'm sorry," she said sincerely. "I didn't mean to treat you as though you were an inanimate object. If it looked like I was making myself at home by being on your bed and using your phone, I'm sorry. This may sound strange, but the minute I came into your house, I felt at home." She saw the surprise in his eyes and went on in spite of it. "It seems natural to be in your house, using your shower, sitting on your bed. If I've over-stepped myself in some way, I apologize."

"I didn't blow up because you made yourself at home, Whitney." His voice sounded weary and strained.

"Then what is it? Why have I made you angry?"

He came to her and cupped her face in his hands. "Do you have any idea how badly I want you? To find you on my bed where I've imagined you was more than I could take."

She raised her hands to cover his. "You have to be aware of how I feel, Stone. I thought my response was fairly obvious earlier in the park. I wouldn't have re-jected you. I'm sorry if I gave you the impression I would."

His thumbs stroked her soft skin. "That wasn't what I was worried about."

"I don't understand."

He led her over to the sofa and with his hands on her shoulders, made her sit down. Standing in front of her, he said, "Since this seems to be the time for plain speaking, I have a question to ask."

"What is it?"

"Have you ever been with a man before?" he asked bluntly.

"What kind of a question is that?" She tried to sound indignant, but it didn't come out the way she wanted.

"A valid one apparently," he said dryly as he noted the color shading her cheeks. "It's one of the things that stops me every time I begin to make love to you."

His words didn't soothe her rising temper. "You make it sound like I have some awful disease. Would you rather I had slept with every sailor in the fleet?"

A muscle jumped in his jaw. "No, I wouldn't like that at all. You're missing the point."

"Which is?"

He crouched in front of her, placing his hands on the sofa on either side of her legs. "Whitney, taking a woman's virginity is a big responsibility for a man, at least it is for me. I know it's an old-fashioned attitude, especially after the way I was brought up, but it's how I feel. I think underneath your carefree attitude about things, you're old-fashioned, too, or you wouldn't still be a virgin."

"Or maybe I was just waiting for you," she said softly.

Blatant desire flared in his eyes and his fingers tightly gripped the soft cushions. "Don't say things like that, Whitney," he said roughly. "I'm trying to do what's right. The man you marry has the right to be the first. Not me. I don't want to hurt you."

He might not want to hurt her, she thought, but he was. His words dealt a fatal blow to her hope for anything permanent between them. He wanted a relationship but only a temporary one. And a platonic relationship as well. For some reason he was determined to wear her like a hairshirt, wanting her but refusing to make love to her. It was a commitment he wasn't ready to make.

Even though she hadn't moved, Stone felt her putting distance between them. She was looking at him, yet he had the feeling she wasn't really seeing him. For a brief moment, something flickered in her eyes, an expression of sadness, of grief, and then it was gone, making him think it had been his imagination. Before he gave in to the impulse to hold her in his arms and comfort her, to hold her until the light came back to her eyes, he abruptly stood up and took several steps away.

When he looked back at her, she hadn't moved. "Say something, dammit!"

Her eyes were dull, their usual liveliness dimmed. "Where's your dryer?"

For a moment, he stared blankly at her. "What?"

She got up and headed for the doorway, pulling his robe securely around her. "I'll get my clothes and then you can show me where the dryer is. As soon as my clothes are dry, I'll have to go home to get ready for the gallery opening."

He raked his hand violently through his hair as he wrestled with his temper, frustration, and bewilderment. "Are you simply going to ignore what we were discussing?"

Her shoulders slumped wearily as she crossed her arms over her chest. She looked strangely dignified in his oversized robe, and she met his gaze squarely. "What good would it do to discuss it? You've made up your mind about what is going to happen between us. Or I should say, what isn't going to happen between us. You've made yourself perfectly clear. You want a nice, safe, chaste relationship without any commitment or intimacy. Nothing I can say will change your mind and I'm not sure I want to at this point."

She tilted her head to one side. "I am curious about one thing though. You're a healthy adult male with all the right equipment and desires. You don't want to have sex with someone you know, so I can't help wondering what you do about it. It's none of my business, of course. It's just that last night you went on about meaningless sex between strangers, so I got the impression it wasn't what you preferred. I'm not exactly a stranger, but you don't want me either."

"You know better than that," he said tartly. "If I didn't want you, we wouldn't be having this conversation in the first place. I also told you why I'm not going to do anything about it."

"Ah, yes. My precious virginity. The operative word here is mine, not yours, by the way." Her hands shifted to her hips, and she glared at him with growing fury. "Even my father at his most autocratic didn't have the nerve to tell me when or if I could ever sleep with a man, other than to give me a vague lecture on the dangers of promiscuous behavior. I've never been with a man because I never wanted to before I met you. It never came up as a matter of discussion because I was never tempted or cared enough for any other man. You stay with your harmless, faceless women, Stone. Find someone else less threatening than I am to have a relationship with, someone with whom you won't have to use the excuse of her virginity to keep you from becoming emotionally involved." Her voice cracked. "It won't be me."

The robe swirled around her legs as she turned and hurried toward his bedroom, but not before Stone caught a glimpse of tears glistening in her eyes. Damn, he cursed silently. All he had wanted to do was protect her, and instead he had hurt her. He was still in shock from hearing her say she cared about him. Her words had opened up a whole host of possibilities he had never even dared hope for. The sound of the bedroom door slamming galvanized him into action.

When he entered the bedroom, his gaze raced around the room. His robe was lying on the bed in a crumpled heap as if it had been thrown there, but there was no sign of Whitney. The door to the bathroom was shut and he started toward it. He had taken only a step when it was yanked open and Whitney came out wearing her wet clothes.

"Whitney, wait."

He reached out a hand to stop her as she stormed past, but she jerked her arm out of his grasp. "Save it," she said rudely. "Either drive me home or call a cab for me. If you won't do either one, I'll walk."

His long strides beat her to the door, and he slammed it shut so she couldn't leave. The loud noise deflated her temper like a pin in a balloon. Defeated, she bowed her head and stared at the floor. She was trembling but he didn't think it was entirely from wearing wet clothes.

"Let me go, Stone." Her voice was thick with unshed tears.

"Not this way."

Gently, he picked her up, carried her over to his bed, and laid her down, shoving the robe onto the floor. He stretched out beside her and cradled her in his arms. He needed to hold her, to comfort her and to soothe his own raw emotions. At first she was stiff and tense against him, but as his hands stroked her back, she began to relax. When she sighed, her warm breath grazed his neck and he loosened his hold on her enough to look down into her face. Her eyes were closed and moisture had dampened her lashes.

"Would it make you feel better if I apologized?" he asked.

Her hair brushed against his cheek as she shook her head.

He couldn't help smiling. She was a stubborn little cuss. "Well, I will anyway. I'm sorry for being such a . . ."

"Jackass," she supplied in a hoarse voice.

"That, too," he agreed dryly. "I did warn you. Caring for someone else is new to me. I've been alone for a long time without considering anyone else's feelings but my own. I'm bound to make mistakes."

He rolled onto his back, bringing her with him. He half expected her to resist and was inordinately pleased when she didn't. Combing his fingers through her curls, he urged her head down onto his shoulder.

He sighed heavily. "If I can keep my foot out of my mouth long enough, are you willing to give me another chance? Or have I used up all my chances with you?"

She propped herself up on one elbow and looked at him. "You get another chance on one condition."

His relief was so overwhelming, he found it difficult to speak. "Which is?" he managed to ask huskily.

"So far all the decisions about how and when and if we have a relationship have been yours. Even whether or not we make love. I've lived under a dictatorship with my father, Stone. I prefer a democracy."

His fingers continued to play with her hair as he said quietly, "I have a lot to learn about you, don't I?"

"And about yourself."

His fingers stilled. "You may have a point there. Are you willing to teach me?"

She smiled. "Are you willing to learn?"

"I'm willing to try. I don't want to lose you."

The gleam of mischief he had missed seeing was back in her eyes. "But you haven't had me yet."

Laughing softly, he pulled her back into his arms and hugged her. "There's no one else like you, Whitney. You amaze me. You also have one helluva temper, lady. I feel as if I've been singed by a tiny flamethrower."

"That's only fair. I feel as if I've been through a wringer."

He fingered her damp shirt. "It doesn't feel like it. Don't you think you'd better get out of those wet clothes?"

She raised an eyebrow. "I think I'd better get off your bed. Our troubles started because I was on your bed."

"Do we get to vote on this? We're supposed to be operating under a democracy, remember?"

"It's very tempting but I don't have time. And you're a man who considers time important, remember? I have this gallery opening to go to tonight, so I'd better go."

"Do I get to vote whether or not I can go with you?"

She looked surprised. "Would you want to? It might be boring for you."

"My lessons have to start sometime."

She smiled. "That's true." She leaned her forearms on his chest and rested her chin on them. "I don't know if you realize it but we've both just had a lesson. An important lesson."

"Have we? I must have missed it. You're the teacher. What was it?"

Her forefinger traced an invisible line across his chest. "We've just had our first fight and our relationship survived it."

He suddenly rolled her over so he was lying half on top of her. He grinned down at her, then brushed his lips lightly over hers. "Aren't we supposed to make up after having a fight?"

"I thought we already did," she said breathlessly.

"Somehow I had a different picture of how people make up." He pushed himself up and slipped off the bed, then held his hand out to her. "I'll concede to the higher authority."

When she was on her feet, he picked up his robe and handed it to her. "Go put this back on and toss those wet clothes out. I'll put them in the dryer. The gallery opening awaits."

She hesitated after taking the robe. "Did you mean it about coming with me?"

"I wouldn't miss it." He studied her face carefully, lifting his hand to touch her cheek. "What time is the opening?"

"Seven, I think."

He smiled at her vague reference to time. "I'll make sure you get there." Shoving the sleeve of his shirt back, he indicated his watch. "I suggest you get a move on."

Giving him a mock salute, she went into the bathroom. Once inside, she leaned against the door and closed her eyes as relief flowed through her. She felt like someone who had been given a reprieve from a death sentence. She had no idea where they were going but for a while anyway, they were going to be together.

Seven

During the next couple of days Whitney and Stone
tried to be together whenever they could manage the
time away from their respective jobs. It wasn't easy
since their work schedules didn't exactly coincide,
mainly because Whitney didn't have one.

The third time Stone had to chase Whitney over half
of San Francisco, he was less than good-natured about
it. He finally caught up with her at a store that sold
tires and car parts. When Melvin had told him she was
at a car parts store, he had thought her VW might be
giving her problems again. But he discovered she was
there to fix an animated figure located in the middle of
the store. Several men were standing around watching
her tinker with a three-foot-high stuffed monkey who
held a wrench in one hand and a small plastic tire in
the other. At the moment the monkey was motionless
and Whitney was on her knees behind it, a soldering
iron in one hand. She was laughing at some remark
one of the men had made.

"Are you enjoying yourself?" Stone asked, a cutting edge to his voice.

She had to peer around the monkey in order to see him clearly. A warm smile appeared on her lips and in her eyes. Then her smile vanished when she saw he was glowering. She sat back on her heels and said regretfully, "I was supposed to meet you at the warehouse."

"At six. It's now a little after seven."

It didn't take a genius to determine he was not pleased to be kept waiting—again. "It won't take me a minute to finish up here and then we can go."

She put down the soldering iron, closed up the back of the monkey, and inserted a plug back into the outlet on the side of the display stand. As soon as she depressed a switch, the monkey's arms and head began to move in synchronization. The men made various comments of approval as she gathered up her tools and put them into the small metal carrying case at her side.

One of the men helped her down off the platform and another picked up the tool case. Stone stepped forward and relieved the men of their hold on Whitney and her tools. He had to whisk her out of the store before he did something stupid, like warn off all those men who outweighed him by at least fifty pounds each. They were only being helpful, yet he still didn't like any other man touching her.

Since she had driven the van to the store, he told her he would follow her back to the warehouse. "Or do you have some other creature that needs your help?"

She shook her head. "I don't have anything else that has to be done tonight." She smiled. "I'm all yours."

He combed his fingers through her hair, then held her head still to kiss her. The kiss was brief and totally unsatisfying, and he lifted his head and stared down into her eyes.

"You're not mine yet," he said gruffly, "but you will be."

Slightly rattled, Whitney had to force herself to concentrate on her driving. Stone had been remarkably patient with her over the last several days, but she had a feeling his patience had been tried once too often. He had made all the compromises and now it was time she compromised. It wasn't as though he was asking a great deal. He wanted to see her, wanted to be with her in the evenings when he was through with work. The problem of her not having any set hours for her own work was interfering with their time together.

Because of the nature of his job, he couldn't very well adjust his schedule to hers. So it was up to her to make a few changes in her work habits. At other times in her life, she had conformed to schedules when it was important, and she could do it again. If she wanted to continue seeing Stone, she was going to have to make a few concessions.

Stone was held up by several stop lights, so Whitney arrived at the warehouse ahead of him. Once inside, he barely greeted Melvin before Whitney grabbed his arm. She led him back to the entrance as though the place were on fire and they had to leave in a hurry.

"What's the rush?" he asked.

"We have things to do," she said, sliding the door shut behind them and starting toward his car.

"Like what?"

She gave him a brilliant smile. "We're going shopping."

The store Whitney had chosen was going to close in a half hour, but she knew what she was looking for and quietly began scanning the contents of the glass display cases.

After his initial shock at the type of store she had dragged him into, Stone grappled with several theories and discarded all of them. He finally said, "Whitney, this is a jewelry store."

She was bending over a glass case, staring down at the items displayed on the shelves. "I know."

"Whitney, those are watches."

She gave him a quelling glance over her shoulder. "I know what they are. I'm going to buy one."

She pointed to a tray of watches, asking the clerk to bring them out for her to examine more closely, then gave a startled cry when she was abruptly turned around to face Stone.

There was a strange catch in his voice when he asked, "Why?"

She met his intent gaze. "Because time is a terrible thing to waste if it keeps me from being with you."

He was gazing at her with an expression that made her throat thick with emotion. Then he pulled her into his arms and simply held her, his arms so tight she could hardly breathe. For a long moment they stayed that way until the clerk cleared his throat pointedly and Stone reluctantly released her.

Turning back to the counter, she gave the watches all her attention. She picked up several and tried them on, but replaced them on the velvet-covered tray, a frown of concentration on her face. The clerk brought out another selection, but she still didn't have any luck finding a watch she could live with. Each one was too gaudy, too ornate, or too expensive. She hadn't realized how difficult it was going to be to select a watch.

But now that she had made up to her mind to purchase one, it had to be just the right one.

In the meantime, Stone had moved over to the next display case and beckoned another clerk to show him something. When the tray was set in front of him, he picked up the one that had caught his attention. Without even glancing at the price tag, he took it back to Whitney and lifted her hand.

"How about this one?" he asked as he slipped the watch on her wrist.

Bending her arm so she could see the watch, she laughed and raised her amused eyes to meet his. "I'll take it."

If the clerk thought it was strange that a man in an expensive business suit was buying a Mickey Mouse watch for his casually dressed lady, he didn't show it. "Would you like your purchase wrapped or will you wear it?" he asked in a bland voice.

"I'll wear it."

The clerk removed the small price tag dangling from the band and told her how much it cost. The price was higher than Whitney had expected, but this watch was the one she wanted.

"Will it be cash or charge?" the clerk asked.

"Charge," Whitney answered, and began to reach into the back pocket of her jeans when Stone said, "Cash."

He already had his wallet out and was laying the money on the counter before she could protest.

"Stone, you don't have to pay for the watch. I can afford it."

His smile was intimate and warm. "You've just given me a gift more valuable than this watch. Let me buy it for you."

"All right. Thank you," she murmured, her own smile a little shaky.

"Perhaps you should ask for a set of instructions to go with the watch so you'll know how it works," Stone drawled as she accepted the receipt and the warranty from the clerk.

"I don't think that's necessary," she said smoothly. "I happen to know someone who's an expert on time. He'll show me how it works."

Laughing, Stone put his arm around her shoulders as they left.

Since they were closer to his house than her apartment, they went there after stopping at a delicatessen on the way. Several times Stone had to admonish Whitney for reaching into the large bag she held on her lap and sampling the corn chips that were on top of the plump sandwiches.

"Are we hungry?" he asked.

"We are starving." She held up her wrist so her watch gleamed in the reflected headlights. "It's way past dinnertime."

"If you eat all the food before we reach my house, you'll have to cook to replace the food you devoured. You *can* cook, can't you?"

"Of course," she replied with as much dignity as possible, considering she had just popped another corn chip in her mouth. "My speciality is cooked goose, so you'd better behave."

Returning his attention to the road, he shook his head. He should know better by now. Then he realized he had a silly grin on his face. It wasn't altogether surprising. He was happy and he knew why. He was with Whitney. She had the rare ability to make the ordinary extraordinary, and he relished every minute he spent with her.

As the garage door was opening, he glanced over and saw her hand descend into the bag again. "If you can control your gluttony for a few more minutes, we can eat in relative style inside."

The style he had in mind was to spread a quilt on top of the Oriental rug in his living room and light a fire in the marble fireplace. The only other illumination was from a small lamp across the room. He was getting the hang of the picnic spirit, and Whitney was oddly touched that it had been his idea.

He removed his coat and tie and turned up his sleeves several turns before sitting down on the quilt. Whitney had kicked off her beat-up tennis shoes and sat cross-legged in front of the tempting bag of food.

He caught her admiring her new watch. "What time is it?"

"Time to eat," she said, and opened the sack.

She handed out the food and there was a companionable silence as they munched away.

"If you had brought out candles," Whitney said casually as she finished her pastrami on rye, "I would suspect you of setting up a seduction scene."

"Candles are out. I spent too many nights trying to do homework by candlelight when the electric bill didn't get paid to consider them a romantic prop." He suddenly reached for her and tumbled her on her back, following her down onto the quilt. "Besides," he murmured, "I don't need candles to seduce you and you certainly don't need them to seduce me."

He lowered his head and kissed her with all the pent-up desire of the last couple of nights when he had settled for brief good-night kisses at her door.

His casual reference to his childhood was forgotten as she gave herself up to the delicious, tormenting feel of his mouth on hers, his chest pressing against her breasts. He eased his leg between her thighs as his hand tugged at her shirt where it was tucked into her jeans.

Suddenly he stopped and began to draw away, but she wouldn't allow it. Her fingers tightened on his arms. "No. Don't stop."

Her arms encircled his shoulders, her fingers sifting through his soft hair. She wanted to lose herself in him, wanted him to transport her to that magical place where they were the only people on earth, where passion was king and they were the loyal subjects.

Perspiration dampened his skin as Stone's mind fought his body's needs. Her scent weakened his good intentions and he groaned, "Whitney, say something to stop me."

"I don't want you to stop," she murmured huskily. "It feels too good."

With a sound of tortured capitulation, he kissed her with a primitive passion. His hand slid under her shirt, seeking her satiny flesh. Her skin was cool to his searing touch. For a moment, he was still as he discovered her breasts were bare of any covering other than the loose shirt. Then he filled his hand with the fullness of her breasts, moaning into her mouth. He thought he would explode as she arched her hips into his.

Breaking away from her mouth, he caressed her throat with his lips. "Whitney, I have to have you. I can't wait any longer."

Her fingers clutched his back. "Neither can I."

At her softly spoken words he lifted his head so he could look into her eyes. "Are you sure?"

"It's time."

Exultation surged through him and he closed his eyes, then he kissed her with a desperation born of uncontrollable need. Somehow he had to rein in his raging hunger so he didn't hurt her, but it wasn't going to be easy. His body was heavy and taut with the desire to bury himself deep inside her, to claim her completely.

As he unbuttoned her shirt, she did the same to his. "Oh, God, Whitney," he muttered when he saw her naked breasts. "I want you so much."

"Is it supposed to ache like this?" she whispered, sliding her hands across the bare expanse of his chest.

"Where does it ache?" He touched her breasts. "Here?"

She shook her head and his hand slid to her waist and beyond. The coarse material guarding the apex of her thighs was no barrier to his intimate touch.

"Or here?" he asked, his voice rough with desire. In answer, her hips arched up violently and she gasped his name.

Aroused to the breaking point, Stone swept away her remaining clothes. As each piece was removed, he asked the same question. Her answer each time was in her eyes and her hands and the way she twisted beneath his touch, searching for more primal pleasure.

At last he tore off his own clothes. For a long moment he let his gaze stroke over her, grasping for his last ounce of control before allowing himself to touch her again. Her lips were moist and parted as she looked up at him. Slowly she lifted her hand toward him in a gesture of trust and impatience. Lying down beside her he pulled her into his arms, trembling as his bare flesh touched hers for the first time. The question of where she ached wasn't asked again. He let his hands and mouth speak for him.

Caressing her hips with his lower body and his hands, he thought he would explode. She duplicated his tantalizing movements by writhing against him, her silken hands flowing over him.

Unable to withstand the throbbing desire shuddering through him, Stone gently pushed her onto her back. His mouth absorbed her gasp of shocked pleasure as his body covered hers, his knee parting her legs. When he lifted his head and gazed down at her, he saw no fear in her glazed eyes, only desire. Using his last remnant of restraint, he slid his arms under her to cushion his weight as he eased into her slowly. Hands under her hips absorbed her sudden jerk as his body invaded hers for the first time.

Even though it was killing him, he held his body still.

"Are you all right?" he asked hoarsely.

She tossed her head restlessly back and forth. He began to withdraw from her, but her hips followed. "It still aches," she said. "Only you can make it stop."

"I'll take care of protecting you," he murmured, moving away from her briefly to do so. Then, with as much tenderness as he could summon, he gave in to the throbbing need to make her his. Locking her firmly to his body, he took her with him, stoking the embers of passion into a blazing inferno.

A rippling explosion consumed them, leaving them breathless and caught up in the magic of incredible ecstasy. It was some time before Stone could find the energy to move. He rolled onto his side, keeping her in the circle of his arms.

As he watched, she slowly opened her eyes and smiled. "And I tried to tell you about picnics."

He made a choking sound that was part amusement and part surprise. "My picnics don't get rained on either."

"But your picnics are more exhausting than mine." Nuzzling his throat, she muttered, "Me and my little Mickey Mouse watch may never move again."

"No problem."

He rose to a kneeling position and swung her into his arms. He carried her into his bathroom and stepped into the shower stall, then let her slide down his body. Keeping an arm around her waist, he turned on the shower spray.

Whitney shrieked.

"What's wrong?" he asked, startled. "Is the water too hot?"

"My watch. It'll get wet."

He couldn't help smiling at the panic in her voice. "Mickey is waterproof."

"Oh, good." She slipped her arms around his neck and went up on her tiptoes to kiss him.

The water sluiced over them, but it didn't quench the spark of awakened desire. Strong hands slid over slippery curves. Now he could take his time to appreciate the shapely lines of her body. His raging hunger had been appeased but his appetite for her was still strong. Lowering his head, he licked the moisture off the gentle slope of first one breast and then the other. Her sigh was faint compared to the sound of running water, yet he heard it and wanted to hear more. He slid his hands over her ribs and down her hips, and his mouth left a heated trail over her stomach. He was rewarded with a yearning sound deep in her throat. She was so beautifully responsive, he thought. It was too soon for her to make love again, but there were other ways to satisfy them both.

It was a night of firsts for Whitney, starting with Stone's exciting lovemaking and ending with spending the night in his bed.

When the alarm woke them the following morning, they learned little things about each other, minor details that came up as they faced the morning after the night together. Their lovemaking had brought them closer physically and emotionally, creating a bond that hadn't been there before. But it was too new to take for granted and neither one expected the change to solve all their problems. There were still vast differences in their lifestyles that one night of passion couldn't dissolve.

Whitney discovered Stone wasn't particularly chatty first thing in the morning, but after a shower and a cup of coffee, he was more sociable. Stone learned Whitney didn't want anything for breakfast except a piece of toast and tea, whereas he preferred the large breakfast he prepared for himself.

Whether it was because she was there or whether it was his normal way of starting the day, he had put on a white shirt and the slacks that went with the suit jacket he had laid out on the made-up bed. He hadn't put on a tie yet but had left his collar open.

Out of habit, Stone turned on the small televison sitting on the kitchen counter to listen to the news while he ate his breakfast. Usually alone, he had the company of the newcaster's voice every morning to fill the silence. This morning, however, the announcer had competition from Whitney. Since he would rather listen to Whitney's voice, he turned off the televison. Crime statistics and bombings in foreign countries couldn't compare with hearing Whitney ramble on about everything from kitchen appliances to questions about where various things were located in his cupboards.

Amazingly enough, after conferring with her new watch, Whitney herself nudged Stone to get a move on or he would be late for work. "You need to drop me off at my apartment so I can change clothes," she said. Giving him a teasing smile, she added, "How would it look to your staff if the boss was late?"

He gazed at her with guarded seriousness. "There's a way to eliminate the trip to your apartment in the mornings. You could leave some clothes here."

Her heart thudded heavily in her chest. She hadn't expected that and wasn't prepared with an answer. "Are you asking me to move in with you?"

A corner of his mouth curved up slightly. "I thought it might be more efficient."

His offer was as much a surprise to him as it was to her. He had never wanted any woman to live with him before, but he wanted Whitney's toothbrush to hang on the rack next to his. He wanted her clothing hanging in the same closet as his. As much time and effort as he had poured into his house, it had been missing some vital ingredient that would make it a home . . . until Whitney had walked into it.

His gaze shifted to her current apparel, which was one of his shirts. "Although I can't complain about what you have on now, I wouldn't want Melvin to see you wearing only my shirt."

While Whitney liked the possessive note in his voice, she didn't think it was wise to take him up on his offer. "Stone," she said hesitantly. "Don't you think that's rushing things a bit?"

"I don't know. I've never asked anyone to move in with me before. What's the usual time to ask a woman to move in with a man?"

"How would I know?" she replied with feeling. "I'm the inexperienced one, remember?"

His smile was slightly off center and held a hint of sensuality. "Not anymore."

A hint of a blush heightened her color. "True, but one night does not an expert make. I still think we're rushing into a deeper commitment than we're ready for."

He shrugged as though it really didn't matter and pushed his chair back. "Maybe you're right." He carried his dishes over to the sink. With his back to her, he said casually, "All I have left to do is put on a tie, so why don't you go get dressed and I'll finish cleaning up the kitchen. Then I'll take you home."

While Whitney dressed, she realized she was disappointed that Stone had dismissed the subject so easily. It was ridiculous because she should be relieved he agreed with her. So why wasn't she? she wondered. Had he asked her to move in with him because he thought that was what she expected? Or did he really want her to live with him? She was so befuddled, she discovered she had buttoned her shirt wrong and had to start all over.

When Stone pulled up to the curb in front of her apartment building, he glanced at his watch. "I'd better not take the time to walk you to your door. If I come by the warehouse tonight, what are the chances you'll be there?"

A flood of relief washed over her. He still wanted to see her. After turning him down, she half expected to be dumped like a pile of dirty laundry on the sidewalk outside her building. Considering she was wearing the same clothes she had on yesterday, the thought had been appropriate.

"Tell me what time you'll be there and I'll make sure I'm there."

His raised eyebrow and skeptical gaze told her he found her promise a little hard to believe. "That hasn't worked so far."

She tapped the crystal face of her watch. "I didn't have Mickey then."

"I think you're asking a lot of a watch but we'll try it. How about seven? I'll go home and change first."

"Fine."

She had her hand on the latch when he stopped her. "Aren't you forgetting something?"

"What?"

His hand cupped the back of her neck and he pulled her toward him. "This," he murmured just before his lips found hers. All too soon, he raised his head and leaned across her to open her door. "See you at seven."

One benefit of having Melvin as a partner was that he was obsessive and self-absorbed with his various designs and rarely noticed much outside of the workshop. It wasn't until late in the afternoon that he happened to catch Whitney shoving back the sleeve of her denim jacket to glance at her wrist.

When he saw her do it again a little later, his curiosity got the better of him. "What's wrong with your wrist?" he asked.

"Nothing's wrong with my wrist."

"You keep looking at it."

"So? It's my wrist."

"I don't recall your ever being so fascinated with it before." He left his chair and walked over to where she was sitting in front of her computer. "You know how I hate to feel left out of things."

He picked her arm up by two fingers as though there might be a chance of it's being contaminated. Then he turned back the cuff of her jacket. "Well, I'll be damned. If it isn't Disneyland's famous mouse. Do I get to guess how he happened to become glued to your wrist, or are you going to tell me?"

She opened her mouth to speak, but Melvin answered his own question before she had a chance to say anything. "Prince Charming bought it, right?"

She couldn't deny it. "But it was my idea."

Giving the watch one more look, he dropped her arm. "It's a mighty cute gift. I lean toward flowers and candy myself. Leave it to the prince to do something different. Is there any particular reason you keep checking the position of Mickey's hands?"

"Stone's coming here around seven. I want to make sure I have these accounts done before then."

"Hmmm. Prince has been a little cranky the last couple of nights when he's either had to wait or had to go hunt you down," Melvin said with amusement. "This sounds serious, Whitney. He's changed you into an organized clock-watcher. I never thought I would see the day. What happened to all those declarations of independence I heard after college?"

"No one is entirely independent, Melvin. I realized that recently. You and I depend on each other to get our designs done on time, and depend on our clients to pay us. We've had to make concessions like losing sleep in order to get our work done to meet a deadline."

He held up his hand. "You don't have to explain. Just don't expect me to change the way I work. Prince Charming didn't buy me any watch."

Whitney laughed and shook her head in amused exasperation. "When we started Grant and Gunn, we never said we couldn't have a private life separate from our business."

"That's true." He took off his glasses and cleaned them with a handkerchief. "I have a feeling it's going to be real interesting around here," he said dryly.

With that understatement, he put his glasses back on and returned to work, accepting the new development with apparent good humor.

When Stone arrived at the warehouse, Whitney had completed her work for the day and was ready to leave with him. Ignoring Melvin's gibe about Mickey bringing her back to work at eight o'clock in the morning, she left the warehouse.

For the rest of the week, she managed to keep to a relatively normal schedule. At least it was normal for Stone. He accepted it as the way she should plan her day, not realizing what a strain it was for her to maintain. He had no idea she was putting twice as much effort into the day as she did before.

By the weekend, she was beginning to feel she wasn't carrying her load at Grant and Gunn. Melvin didn't complain, even though on Thursday night he ended up taking down a display by himself after a store was closed. Many of their clients preferred to have such work done after hours so the normal routine of their business wouldn't be disrupted. Since she wasn't there to help him, it took him twice as long to get the job done.

Being with Stone each evening was becoming the most important part of Whitney's day. If a few sacrifices had to be made, then she would make them. She wanted to be with him as much as she could, to store up as many memories as possible. She prided herself on being a realist. On the day of Sylvia's wedding he had made it clear he wasn't interested in marriage, and she wasn't expecting anything permanent with Stone.

Whatever she had to do to make their relationship last for as long as possible, she would do.

Eight

The pressure began to tell on Whitney by the end of the following week. Her life was becoming divided into sections and they were beginning to overlap. Worse, the strain of trying to keep to a schedule, to compress her creative drive into an alien eight-hour day, was fostering a restlessness and dissatisfaction within her that resulted in difficulty sleeping. She lay awake beside Stone, going over in her mind the schematics of a design she was creating. Ideas came to her at odd moments, and before, she had been able to put them into form whenever they popped up. That was the way she had worked best. Her imagination wasn't like a machine that could be turned on and off; it wasn't disciplined to work in a structured period of time.

The ticking of the clocks in Stone's home became an irritant that grated against her nerve endings. They were like metronomes telling her she had to match the rhythm set by the beat of time.

Stone, blissfully unaware of her inner struggle, was

more than satisfied with the way their relationship was progressing. Occasionally they took in a movie or went out to dinner, but he preferred the quiet nights when they prepared dinner at his house and watched televison or talked, ending the evening in his bed. For a man who had never had any sort of home life, having Whitney with him in his house was the nearest he had ever come to a close relationship.

It never occurred to him that Whitney wasn't as happy with the arrangement as he was.

On Friday, Whitney stopped by her apartment after taking down a display. It had been several days since she had checked the messages on her answering machine, so she rewound the tape and listened while she gave her plants a badly needed watering.

She almost dropped the watering can when she heard the imperious tones of her father's voice emanating from the answering machine.

"Whitney, your mother and I are in San Francisco until Saturday, the twenty-first. We will be free on Friday evening, the twentieth. Call the Airport Hilton and leave a message if you wish to have dinner with us in the city."

She walked over to the answering machine and rewound the tape so she could listen to her father's message again to make sure she had heard correctly. She had. Her parents expected to see her that evening.

"Terrific," she muttered. Just what she needed was another complication.

Checking the time, she grimaced as she realized she was consulting her watch almost as often as Stone did. In four hours, she was supposed to meet him at his office to go to dinner. Now she was going to have to change those plans.

She flipped through her address book and found the number for Hamilton and Associates. The phone was answered after the first ring and she was immediately put through to Stone. Since she had never called him before at his office, his first question was perfectly natural.

"What's wrong?"

"I won't be able to meet you later," she said bluntly.

"Why not?" He sounded unconcerned.

She quickly explained about the message from her father. "I have to call the hotel now and make arrangements to have dinner with them tonight."

"Tell your father we'll arrive at the hotel at seven," Stone said matter-of-factly. "The Hilton has a fine restaurant and they won't have to make the trip into the city. Unless they would rather go to another restaurant. Whatever is easiest for them."

Shock kept her from saying anything right away. He was taking it for granted he was included in her plans for the evening. "Stone," she started thinly, then stopped to take a deep breath. "I'm not sure you would enjoy having dinner with my parents. It won't exactly be a picnic."

His chuckle was low and provocative. "I've grown quite fond of picnics, Whitney, especially the last one we had in my living room. But I prefer to have our picnics alone. I think we'd better settle for a nice respectable restaurant."

"You don't have to come with me, Stone."

He paused as though thinking over what she said. Finally, he asked sharply, "Is it that you don't want me to meet your parents or you don't want them to meet me?"

Whitney slumped down onto one of the bar stools,

her fingers clenching the phone. "You're misunderstanding me, Stone. Having dinner with them is not going to be one of the highlights of the week, but I'm obligated because they are my parents. You don't have to waste the evening having dinner with them."

"I have to meet them sometime, Whitney," he said, and the coolness was gone from his voice. "It might as well be tonight. I'll pick you up at your apartment at six-thirty."

Whether he didn't want to hear any more arguments or whether he had nothing else to say, she was left holding a dead phone. She set the receiver down, her mind replaying what he had said about having to meet her parents sometime. She didn't understand what he meant, but she didn't have time to dwell on his statement right now. She had another phone call to make.

Her parents weren't in their room, so she left a message that she would arrive at the hotel at seven and would bring a guest. Then she stabbed at the buttons on the phone again and waited for Melvin to answer. It didn't take long to tell him she wouldn't be returning to the warehouse that day. But then he reminded her of the deadline closing in on them for the completion of the dragon display.

Stone wasn't going to like it, she thought as she hung up the phone, but she was going to have to spend some of the weekend at the warehouse. It wasn't fair to expect Melvin to continue doing all the work. She couldn't pretend indefinitely to Stone and to herself that they could go on this way. He had to either accept that her work was important to her or . . . Well, she would face that when the time came.

But first she had to get through the upcoming dinner.

• • •

To Whitney's amazement, the evening with her parents wasn't the ordeal she thought it was going to be. After his initial surprise that the fourth member of the party was a man, her father set out to become better acquainted with Stone. He was obviously pleased when he learned Stone was more than respectably employed with a business of his own.

The admiral's military bearing kept him erect in his chair, refusing to bow even slightly to age. He was a large man, tall, thick in the shoulders, his hair more white than grey. He wore authority like a coat. He was a man used to respect and deference, yet not overly generous in giving the same to those he met until they earned them. His eyes were a piercing blue, cool and judgmental.

More than once, Whitney saw her father glance from her to Stone and back again with a gleam of approval in his eyes. For once it seemed she had done something right in her father's estimation, even if he was putting the wrong connotation on Stone's being with her.

Whitney's small frame came from her mother, who sat like a delicate kitten next to her lion of a husband. Like Whitney, she gave the impression of delicacy, while underneath, she had a quiet toughness that had enabled her to hold her own against the admiral's strong personality.

Whitney mentally squirmed as her mother directed a less than subtle inquisition at Stone, but he sidestepped the more personal questions with ease. He managed to satisfy the parental curiosity without actually giving out his complete life history.

To take some of the heat off Stone, Whitney asked her parents why they were in San Francisco.

"It was time for your father's yearly physical," her mother said. "The doctor he had gone to in San Diego was transferred to Oaknoll Naval Hospital in Oakland. The doctor's wife and I went shopping and sightseeing while your father was at the hospital yesterday."

"Have you received the results of your physical?" Whitney asked her father.

He brushed off her concern brusquely. "I'm as healthy as ever. All the tests were normal."

"I'm not a bit surprised," she said dryly. No disease would dare attack the admiral.

Stone almost smiled when Whitney's mother interjected a casual comment about having lunch at a restaurant near Lake Merritt. During the evening, he had noticed how several times Marion Grant had stepped in verbally to defuse a series of brief snipings between her husband and daughter. He was also aware of the strain in the older woman's eyes each time. The dinner with Whitney's parents wasn't at all what he had expected. He was the outsider at the table, but the other three were the ones who were tense and ill at ease, and it had nothing to do with him.

At one point the admiral mentioned his irritation that he had to leave a message instead of talking with Whitney personally when he called her apartment.

"I purposely phoned late in the evening when I thought you would be home. I could understand your having to put in extra hours when you first started your business, but I was hoping you would have become more organized by this time." He turned to Stone and continued, "With your experience in time management, I would think you could give her some pointers on how to better plan her day. She might have more success if she treated her job with some seriousness and learned some proper business techniques."

Even though the admiral's voice held a note of censure, Stone didn't take offense. Out of the corner of his eye, he caught a glimpse of Marion Grant leaning forward to rush in to fill yet another breach, but he saved her the trouble.

He calmly met the older man's gaze. "Whitney's business is extremely successful, which is why she has to put so much time into it. The reason she wasn't home when you called was because she was with me."

Her father looked astounded but Whitney wasn't sure it was due to her being with Stone or her business being successful. She didn't have to wait long to learn which it was.

"Is this true, Whitney?" her father asked her.

She smiled thinly. "Which part? That my business is successful?"

He nodded abruptly.

"Yes, it's true. Melvin and I have almost more work than we can handle."

"Why didn't you tell us? You know we would have been relieved to hear you're doing well with your . . . ah, work. Frankly, I can't see how your mechanical things could be in much demand."

Marion Grant paled and her hands gripped the edge of the table. Whitney crossed her arms over her chest, her eyes flashing like blue diamonds.

Before either woman could speak, Stone asked, "Have you ever seen any of Whitney's designs, Admiral?"

"No, I can't say I have."

"You should. Each creature I've seen is cleverly constructed. Whitney and her partner give pleasure to young children, businessmen, truck drivers, housewives, whoever sees the displays they design. From a rabbit to a dragon to a nativity scene, they decorate, entertain, and advertise in a unique way. There aren't many people who can do what Whitney and Melvin do with metal and wire. They use state-of-the-art equipment that I would need instructions just to turn on."

To say her father was speechless was putting it mildly. The older man stared at Stone for several moments, then he turned his head to gape at his daughter as though he had never seen her before. In a way, Stone mused, he really hadn't. The admiral had his preconceived ideas of who he thought Whitney was, but he hadn't even been close—as he was discovering.

Whitney was surprised by Stone's defense. She could have told him it wouldn't do any good, but she appreciated his efforts anyway. When she glanced at him, he was smiling faintly, waiting for her father's reaction.

The admiral cleared his throat. He stared intently at Whitney, his expression fierce enough to make a seasoned sailor cringe. "Why haven't you told us about your work? Why do we have to hear these things from a stranger?"

"I did try to explain, Father. When I graduated from college and told you what I was going to do, you weren't exactly interested in listening at that time or anytime since."

Rarely did anyone criticize the admiral and his chest heaved with indignation. But Whitney's mother knew the signs of an impending explosion. She had had over thirty years of experience in dealing with her husband's temper, and all she had to do was lay her hand on his arm and keep it there with subtle pressure. It had a magical effect of calming a furious war-horse into a reasonably docile stallion.

"Our flight isn't until the afternoon tomorrow," she said. "Perhaps we could see some of the things you've been making."

It was clear by their similar frowning expressions that neither the admiral nor Whitney thought much of the idea, but Stone and Whitney's mother were in perfect accord. In fact they set about making plans for the next morning as though it was perfectly natural for them to do so.

Looking toward Marion Grant, Stone offered, "I can drive you to the warehouse around ten, and bring you back in plenty of time for your flight."

Marion smiled, the relief in her eyes apparent. "Ten o'clock will be fine. It's very nice of you to offer to drive us. We could take a taxi, but it would be much more comfortable going with you."

Whitney leaned forward to protest. Before she could utter one word, she felt Stone's hand on her thigh and her mouth snapped shut. She was as effectively shushed as her father had been when her mother had touched his arm. If her mind hadn't been on her parents' upcoming visit to the warehouse, she would have wondered about that.

She sat back and took the role of spectator as Stone and her mother finished making the arrangements for the inspection of her work premises. There didn't seem to be anything she could do about it at the moment, aside from making a scene. That wouldn't accomplish anything other than to hurt her mother's feelings. Stone might be acting in what he thought were her best interests, but he didn't understand that she had wanted the first move to come from her father.

During the drive home from the Hilton, Whitney sat silently, gazing at the cars ahead of them on the freeway. It had been a strange evening and she was trying to sort it out. Previous visits with her parents had been uncomfortable on both sides, which was why she rarely attempted to see them. Knowing her father was disappointed with her choice of career and that her mother was uncomfortable with their constant disputes, Whitney found it easier to talk to her mother on the phone rather than subject them all to the tension caused by a visit. Usually she and her father got into heated arguments that ended in stalemates. She could never convince him she was doing what she was doing because she liked it, rather than choosing her occupation out of spite because it irritated him.

At least they hadn't gotten into a full-fledged argument tonight, she thought. In the past her mother had acted as referee between her husband and daughter, but tonight Marion had an assistant. Whitney wondered if Stone realized it.

As the lights of San Francisco's skyline came into view, he said, "You're awfully quiet. Was being with your parents that bad?"

"Why did you invite them to the warehouse tomorrow?" she asked. Her voice was unusually flat.

"It's time they see what you do."

"There have been plenty of other opportunities when they could have seen what I do if they were interested."

"Maybe they were waiting to be asked."

Something in his voice made her look closely at him. He sounded vaguely disapproving. "It's not quite that simple."

"I could see that for myself tonight. I could also see how you and your father are tearing your mother apart."

"You don't know what you're talking about," she said stiffly.

"So why don't you explain it to me?"

Whitney looked away. That was a good question. Why didn't she explain it? The answer was another question. What was there to explain? Unless Stone had lived under the admiral's iron thumb, there was no way he could understand.

She hadn't been paying attention to where they were going, and when Stone pulled off the road and parked the car, she looked around. She saw the distinctive silhouette of the Cliff House in the distance and asked, "Why have we stopped at Ocean Beach?"

"I feel like walking on the beach." Without any further explanation, he opened his door and came around to the car to open hers.

Her mauve knit skirt, white silk blouse, and long sweater coat had been fine for dining in a restaurant, but weren't very appropriate for walking on the beach. As she got out of the car, the wind off the ocean whipped her hair and skirt around violently. She pulled the edges of her sweater coat together and hugged herself.

Stone took her arm and led her toward the beach. When they reached the sand, he moved between her and the ocean to shield her from the buffeting wind. He slid his arm around her waist to pull her against him.

Their shoes sank into the sand with each step as they strolled just above the surf line. The waves collapsing on the beach were the only sound other than the wind.

Whitney didn't realize how tense she had been all evening until she began to relax. The wind was blowing away the anxiety that had her muscles in knots, and she lifted her face to the salty breeze.

Stone felt the tension ease from her body and looked down at her. "Feeling better?"

"Better than what?"

"Better than you felt during the last couple of hours. If you had sat any straighter at the table, you would have snapped your spine."

She gazed out over the ocean. "Being around my father makes me feel like I'm six years old and I've just broken his favorite putter."

The subtle movement of her slender hips as she walked was tightening his body with heat and need. Thoughts of how his hands had held her arching hips as he entered her moist body momentarily clouded his mind. Dropping his arm from her waist, he turned the lapels of his suit coat up against the wind and jammed his hands into his pockets.

"Don't you think it's time you and your father worked out your differences?" he asked.

"You sound like my mother." She stopped walking and stepped in front of him, forcing him to stop too. "By the way, I'd like to state just for the record that I don't appreciate your getting together with my mother to force my father to come see what type of work I do."

"After meeting your father, I can't imagine anyone making him do anything he didn't want to do. If he didn't want to come, he wouldn't." He rested his forearms on her shoulders. "Your mother knows your father pretty well. I only met him tonight, but I got the impression he wants to see where you work, yet he would be the last person to say so."

"You seem to have become an authority on my father after only a couple of hours."

It was too dark for him to be able to see her eyes clearly, and he couldn't tell from her voice whether she was defensive or just plain angry. "I would like to understand what's going on between you and your father. There's more to it than your father's not approving of your choice of career. Why don't you simply explain it to me instead of taking verbal swipes at me?"

It was obvious he wasn't going to give up. She could think of warmer, more comfortable places to have their conversation, but she might as well get it over with.

"You know most of it. In my father's eyes, what I do isn't very dignified or feminine. I understood his reaction in the beginning, but I thought he would eventually accept it. He hasn't."

"What about your mother's reaction?"

She moved away and Stone didn't try to stop her. "My mother was stuck in the middle as usual. She's always been supportive in her own quiet way, but she doesn't fight my battles with Father. My mother has always been more of a mediator than a contestant." Wrapping her sweater tighter around her, Whitney added dryly, "She can manage one stubborn member of the family, but two pigheaded idiots is too much, even for her."

"After seeing you and your father together, I can see her problem. I still think it's time to end this strange feud between the two of you. Tomorrow could be a start in that direction if you meet him halfway."

"One trip to my warehouse isn't going to make that much difference, Stone. He's still determined for me to get a 'regular job,' as he calls it. For over a year a representative from NASA has been coming once a month to Grant and Gunn to offer me a position where I can put my education to more scientific use. The rep is a retired navy captain my father has known for years. Last month I was approached with an offer from a company in Silicon Valley. Not Melvin, who is more talented and has more credentials than I. Only me. When I asked point-blank how this particular computer company knew about me, he told me the man who sent him was Anton Spears. A few more questions later the mystery was solved. At one time Anton Spears was an executive officer aboard an aircraft carrier at, coincidentally, the same time as Admiral Stewart Grant."

From the light of the moon's reflection off the water and sand, she caught the surprise on Stone's face. "My father hasn't given up, Stone. He's calling in a few favors in the hope of persuading me to change my career. Does that sound like a man who is willing to accept what I do?"

"I still think it's worth a try to patch things up between you and your father."

"And you think *I'm* stubborn," she murmured. "Why does this mean so much to you?"

He raked his fingers through his wind-tossed hair. "I don't pretend to be an expert on fathers or families, but I do know if I had them, I wouldn't want to be alienated from them. Your father isn't perfect, Whitney, but he's the only father you have. You expect him to unconditionally accept what you do, yet you can't accept him the way he is. The common ground you have to work from is your relationship as father and daughter."

Stone knew his voice was harsh, and saw that her eyes had widened as she stared up at him. Still he went on. "If you don't consider your relationship with your father worth working for, it makes me wonder how much you're willing to put into ours."

She looked as though she had been struck. Her face was pale in the ethereal glow of the moonlight shining off the water, and her eyes appeared darker and full of pain. Then she seemed to gather herself together, as a shutter fell down over her face and eyes.

He saw her shiver uncontrollably as an exceptionally cool breeze drifted by them. His expression softened, and he wrapped his suit coat around her as he drew her into his warmth.

"This thing between you and your father needs to be resolved, Whitney. It would be a shame to stay at odds with your family. There has to be a way to work out some sort of compromise."

An overwhelming sadness added to her depression when she thought of Stone without a family of his own. He was right. She should try one more time to meet her father halfway. Knowing her father's pride and stubborness, there were no guarantees she would be successful, but Stone had provided her with a chance and she was going to take it. Not only for the sake of her relationship with her father, but because she had to prove to Stone that she didn't give up on someone she cared about.

She had to warn him all his efforts might be in vain, though. "Sometimes we can't always have what we want."

He lowered his head and his lips found the vulnerable hollow of her throat. "And sometimes if we're real lucky, we *can* have what we want. Right now I want you." If her body was all she would give him, he would take it.

His mouth ground against hers with desperate hunger, parting her lips to taste the moist warmth inside. Strong hands stroked down her back and clenched in her rounded bottom, pulling her hard against his aroused body.

She slid her hands around his waist to his back as she arched her hips against his, fitting their bodies together intimately and naturally. A soft sound of desire came from deep in her throat and vibrated around them. Waves of need crashed over her, as strong, as irreversible as the surf breaking onto the sand nearby. There was a roaring in her ears that had nothing to do with the ocean's dynamic power. Every other thought was crowded out by the passion building up inside her.

Their clothes became a hated barrier, their location inconvenient for the demands their bodies were making. Stone lifted his head and stared down at her for a long moment, then he tucked her into his side and started walking back to his car.

Nine

The darkness was changing to the foggy light of dawn as Whitney slowly and carefully slipped out from under Stone's arm without waking him. It took her several minutes to find her clothes, which had been discarded in haste when they had returned last night. In the bathroom she dressed quickly, ran a brush through her hair, and splashed cold water on her face. Shutting off the light, she opened the bathroom door.

Stone was sprawled on his stomach with his arm stretched out across the space she had occupied a few minutes ago. The sheet had slid down to his waist exposing the wide expanse of his back. He looked alone and oddly vulnerable in the bed, and an unfamiliar pain clamped around Whitney's heart.

After they had made love, she had remained awake beside him, thinking over everything he had said on the beach. He feared she had given up on her father. Because of his experiences with his own mother, he hated the thought that she would take the easy way out by running away from the responsibility of a relationship. If she could do it with her father, she could do it with him. Somehow she had to prove to him she was not the type of woman who would abandon him as his own mother had done.

She quietly opened the door and left the bedroom.

An hour later, Stone's hand slid over the sheet searching for Whitney's warm body. When he found only cold sheets and an empty pillow, he slowly opened his eyes. Propping himself upon one arm, he looked toward the bathroom and found the door open, the room beyond dark and unoccupied. He tossed back the sheet and reached for his jeans.

He headed for the kitchen but she wasn't there. She had made a pot of coffee and it was still hot, so she hadn't been gone long. He poured himself a cup of coffee and leaned against the counter, a frown creasing his brow.

Where in hell was she? he wondered as a sliver of fear jabbed him. Had he driven her away? Made too many demands without having the right to issue them? Since he had no experience to draw from, he had acted out of instinct when he'd pressured her into mending the rift in her relationship with her father. Once that was settled, she could concentrate on her relationship with him.

The coffee scalded his tongue, but it was nothing compared to the pain he would feel if he had been wrong about her. He had to know if she would fight for someone she cared about. The easy way out of a situation was to run away from it or to ignore it, and he didn't want to believe she was the type who would do either.

Leaving the kitchen, he heard the Westminster chimes

of the clock in the living room. He automatically glanced at his wrist, but he wasn't wearing his watch. He walked into the living room and glanced at the clock. It was only a little after seven. It was obvious she had left, but how? Her car was parked in front of her apartment.

His hand slid into the front pocket of his jeans and found nothing, then he remembered he hadn't been wearing the jeans last night. Going swiftly into the bedroom, he set his cup down on the bedside table. His slacks were on the floor where he had tossed them last night in his rush to remove his clothes. He shoved his hand into one pocket and then the other, and came up empty-handed.

He didn't need to look in the garage for further evidence. She had taken his car. But where had she gone? If she had simply wanted to leave, she could have called a taxi to take her home. Instead she had confiscated his car. That effectively stopped him from driving to the airport hotel to pick up her parents. It also meant she would have to return to his house.

Still holding his slacks in his tight fist, he sank down onto the bed. After staring into space for what seemed like hours but was actually only a few minutes, he got off the bed and hung up his slacks. Needing something to do, he picked up the rest of his clothes and made his bed. Then he reached for his watch on the bedside table.

His hand froze in the air several inches from the top of the table. A piece of white paper was folded and wrapped around his watch. Separating the paper from the watch, he unfolded it. In clear black ink, Whitney had printed: *No need to pick up my parents. I'm taking care of it. Love, Whitney. P.S. I hope you don't need your car for a while.*

Shock kept him staring at the note, rereading the four-letter word she had printed before signing her name. He slowly folded the note and slid it into his back pocket. Absently, he slipped his watch onto his wrist, his mind going over various things he would like to do to Miss Whitney Grant when he got his hands on her. It looked like he was going to have plenty of time to decide which he would choose.

The chimes of the clock were ringing eleven times when Stone heard the humming sound of the garage door opening. He was just taking a beer out of the refrigerator. He flipped open the tab, leaned a shoulder against the doorway between the kitchen and the garage, and took a healthy swallow.

After opening the door, Whitney came charging in and nearly collided with him, almost dropping the two bags she held in her arms.

"Good Lord, Stone. You scared the life out of me. Why are you standing there?"

"This is my house. I can stand wherever I want to."

The bags were heavy and she went past him into the kitchen to set them down on the counter. As she began to empty the contents of the bags, she glanced over at him. He had reversed his position and was now facing her as he continued to lean against the doorframe. His gaze swept over her, noting her change in clothes.

She had gone back to her apartment and she was wearing a short denim jacket over a white cotton camisole and a denim skirt.

He took another drink of beer, and she raised her brows. "It's a little early for that, isn't it?"

He pushed himself away from the doorjamb. "It's been a long day."

"It's only eleven in the morning."

"It seems later." He walked over to her and peered at the groceries. "What's all this?"

"It's called food."

"Can you put it away and talk at the same time?"

She opened a cupboard and set a container of coffee on the shelf. "Sure. What do you want to talk about?"

He slammed the beer down onto the counter, and some of the liquid sloshed over onto the tiled surface. He stopped her from delving into the bag again by gripping her wrist. "Stop filling the cupboards, Mother Hubbard, and talk to me. I want to know why you took off so early this morning and what you've been doing." And what she had meant by the word love in her note.

Whitney's head jerked around and she stared at him. What she had mistaken for humor was actually quiet rage. "I was going to get around to that after lunch."

He drew her away from the counter to the table. Yanking out a chair with his free hand, he sat down and pulled her onto his lap. "Get around to it now."

His arms were holding her securely, so she had no choice but to stay where she was. She brought her arm up to rest across his shoulders. "This isn't how I wanted to do this. Are you sure you wouldn't rather wait until we have lunch?"

"Whitney." Her name came out as a growl, not a word. "I think I'm showing remarkable restraint by not throttling you for stealing my car and leaving without telling me. I can't promise how long it will last."

"All right. All right," she said grumpily. "After thinking about what you said last night when we were walking on the beach, I called my father early this morning and asked to meet him alone. I thought it best to leave my mother out of it since this was just between my father and me. He's gotten up at five o'clock every morning since I could remember, so I knew he would be awake. I took him to the warehouse, gave him a tour, and then took him back to the hotel."

She didn't go any further, and Stone said, "That explains why you needed my car, but it leaves a big gap in what happened between you and your father."

"Not much," she muttered, staring down at her hand in her lap.

He cupped the back of her neck to bring her head up around to face him. "Whitney, you're going to have to elaborate a little."

Meeting his gaze squarely, she gave him the details he wanted. "I showed him the whole warehouse. Every past, present, and future design. I opened up the cabinets and showed him some of the completed figures and how they worked. I explained how we use computers in the designing stage and in our bookkeeping. Melvin even ran through the complicated movements for the dragon, which is only half ready. My father's sole comment on the way back to the hotel was that everything he saw was interesting, which doesn't say much. I find the mating rituals of the scorpion interesting, but that doesn't mean I'm impressed with the end result."

Stone saw how difficult it was for her to admit failure in explaining to her father the value of her work. Still, he wasn't sorry he had insisted she go through with the attempt in the first place. She had told him it probably wouldn't do any good, but he had wanted her to try.

His fingers lightly played with the loose curls at her neck. "Perhaps your father was more impressed than you thought. He isn't the type of man to gush compliments all over the place." She looked away, and he tugged one of the curls gently to bring her gaze back to his. "You told me once that after the admiral met the President of the United States, he described the meeting as informative. From what I saw of him last night, your father is a man of few words."

Whitney considered what Stone had said. "He did look at everything I showed him without revealing any impatience or boredom, so at least he now knows exactly what I do."

"It's a start."

"Speaking of starts," she said as she slipped off his lap. She reached into a sack and took out a head of lettuce. "I was going to start lunch."

The chair scraped across the floor as Stone shoved it back under the table. "What is this sudden preoccupation with lunch? I usually have to drag you to the table for meals."

She took a bowl out of a cupboard and began tearing the lettuce into small pieces. "I wanted to have lunch with you before I go back to the warehouse," she said as casually as she could.

His hand covered hers and she was forced to stop ripping up the lettuce. "Wait a minute. You're going back to the warehouse today?"

She sighed heavily and kept her eyes down. She knew he wasn't going to like it, but she was going to have to make him accept it. "I have to, Stone."

"Why?" He bent his head in order to see her face more clearly. "It's Saturday. I thought we were going to spend the day together."

She wiped her hands on a towel. Lunch was going to have to wait. "There's a deadline coming up. Melvin has been doing more than his share this past week and we've fallen behind. If we're going to make the deadline, I have to be there to help. Grant and Gunn Animations is my business too."

"How long will it take?"

"It's hard to say. It depends on if we run into any glitches along the way. So far the design is going according to Melvin's plans, but there's still a lot of wiring that has to be done before the dragon is completed."

"You're saying you're going to work all weekend," he said heavily, not looking at her.

"And possibly the rest of the week. The deadline is Friday." When Stone continued to stare into space without saying anything, she added quietly, "I did warn you this might happen."

He turned to her, his expression unreadable. "Yes, you did, but that was before we got involved. I thought you worked all different hours because you had no reason to keep regular hours."

She put her hand on his arm, feeling the tension under her fingers. "Stone, I've tried to keep to the same schedule you do so we could spend time together, but it wasn't fair to make Melvin carry his load and mine too. I was wrong to let you think I would always be able to work the way I did last week."

His eyes were guarded, his voice tightly controlled. "Is this your way of saying it's over between us?"

Her answer was a shocked gasp. "No!"

Moving away from her, he gestured toward the sacks on the counter and the salad bowl. "The condemned man gets a hearty meal? Was that the reason you bought all these groceries?"

"I'm only going to the warehouse to work. I'm not leaving the country. You're misunderstanding me."

"You'll have to explain what it means then, Whitney." His voice was low and slightly rough, as though anger was simmering just under the surface. "Only last night you slept in my bed and made love to me. This morning you left me a note signed 'Love, Whitney,' and now you're telling me you have to go to work and don't know when you'll be free. You'll have to put it down to male stupidity if I don't understand what the hell you're trying to tell me."

Whitney's gaze was caught by the haunted shadows in his eyes. Her chest tightened painfully as she realized he thought she was abandoning him completely, dropping him out of her life as cruelly and as abruptly as his mother had so long ago.

She didn't attempt to touch him. Her words would have to make contact with him. She only hoped she could find the right ones. "Stone, what I'm trying to say is I want it all. I want to spend time with you and yet fulfill my obligation to Melvin and our business. The problem is I haven't figured out how to do that yet without shortchanging one or the other. Last week I selfishly neglected my work so I could be with you. Now I have to help Melvin, and that means I can't spend much time with you. If there is a solution to how I can do both at once, I haven't found it."

Stone felt as though a heavy weight had been lifted off his chest. He didn't like the fact that he couldn't be with her for a while, but it was better than the alternative.

He rolled up his sleeves and washed his hands, then he proceeded to tear up some more lettuce.

She stared at him in astonishment. "What are you doing?"

"I'm helping you fix lunch. The quicker you get to the warehouse, the quicker you'll be through."

"You don't mind?"

"Hell, yes, I mind," he said with feeling. "While I'm waiting for you to finish the dragon, I'm going to come up with a solution so this doesn't happen again. I'd be a lousy effi—"

He wasn't able to finish what he was going to say for the simple reason that Whitney was kissing him. One second he had his hands full of lettuce and the next second, he had his hands full of Whitney.

After thoroughly enjoying the unexpected kiss, he drew her arms down from his neck and asked, "What was that for?"

"For being so understanding. For being you."

His hands moved from her arms to her waist. "As much as I would like to continue this, it's not getting you to the warehouse or getting your work done."

"I told Melvin I would be back at one o'clock. We still have time for lunch."

"Or we could use the time we would take eating lunch for something else," he murmured, bending his head to taste the delicate skin of her throat. "A week is a long time."

"You can still come to the warehouse," she said softly, closing her eyes as she absorbed the delicious shivers of reaction. "I won't be in quarantine."

Stone's breathing was ragged and heavy, his hands urgent and strong as they moved over her back, pulling her against his hard body. "You might as well be, with Melvin there."

She leaned into him and slid her hands under his shirt, reveling in the way the muscles in his back contracted under her palms. She gloried in the knowledge she could make this man tremble with a touch. "I won't be able to do this, will I?" she murmured, her voice soft and sultry.

He shook his head. "And I won't be able to do this." He took her mouth with a hunger that hadn't diminished since he'd met her. An impatient sound came from deep inside him, and he shifted their positions until he was leaning against the counter with his legs spread enough to allow her room between them. His hands clamped down on her hips to bring her lower body intimately against his, and the soft sound of arousal from her lips undermined his control.

"How in hell am I going to get through the next week without this?" he muttered against her mouth.

She crushed her breasts against his chest as she tightened her arms around his neck. "I'm here now."

His eyes were dark with naked longing. "So you are." Suddenly he scooped her up in his arms and carried her into his bedroom.

He set her down by the bed and his hands framed her face. "Did you mean what you wrote in your note?"

She was so wrapped up in the passion he aroused in her, it took her a few seconds to comprehend what he had asked. She didn't need to ask which part of the note he was referring to. Meeting his intense gaze, she spoke softly but seriously. "I meant it. I love you."

Green flames lit up his eyes at her words. He pulled her into his arms, holding her so tightly, her ribs felt crushed. His mouth found hers, sealing her vow of love in a passionate kiss that lingered on her lips even after he raised his head.

His voice was raw with emotion. "Whitney, I don't know if what I feel for you is love." He saw her wince and quickly went on to erase the momentary pain in her eyes. "I know you're the first thought I have in the morning and the last one I have at night. I never knew how empty I was until you filled me with your warmth.

I feel whole and complete only when I'm with you, when I'm inside you, when I'm touching you. If that's love, then I love you too."

Tears glistened in her eyes, and he groaned roughly. "Don't, darling. I can't stand seeing you cry."

"I was so scared,' she said shakily.

His thumbs brushed the moisture from her lashes. "Why?"

"I was afraid you wouldn't accept that I have to work."

He began inching the hem of her camisole from the waistband of her skirt. "I don't like it, but only because I won't be able to be with you the way I want." His mouth brushed hers, his breath warm against her skin. "We'll work it out."

Her bare flesh was like silk under his roaming hands. "We'll work it out together," he repeated.

"Together," she echoed as her fingers went to the buttons of his shirt.

The gamble she had taken had been necessary but frightening, and she had won. His declaration of love freed her as she proceeded to give herself completely in her love for him, knowing she was loved in return.

For the next several days, Whitney worked with Melvin on the dragon, giving her complete attention to the job. They broke only for the occasional times when Stone brought them food. Soldering irons were set aside briefly while they dug into cardboard cartons containing chinese food. Schematic drawings were perused as they absently munched on juicy hamburgers and french fries. The metal framework of the large dragon was the centerpiece as they set crosslegged on the platform devouring fried chicken.

As far as Stone could tell the partners were making progress. He made sure they had food but otherwise left them alone. He had settled into his own routine of sitting in Whitney's old leather chair at her desk, either reading or going over papers he had brought with him from his office. Twice he had caught Whitney dead on her feet. Instead of allowing her to fall asleep on one of the workbenches as Melvin had, he carried her to his car and took her back to her apartment.

When she awoke, he gently shoved her into the shower, made her eat something, and took her back to the warehouse. The demands of his own job kept him from insuring she was taking care of herself all the time, however.

Wednesday evening he went home after work to change clothes, then picked up their dinner. When he arrived at the warehouse, he found her asleep in the leather chair, her feet, encased in her favorite old tennis shoes, propped up on the desk. It took a great deal of willpower to leave her there instead of scooping her up in his arms and taking her to bed.

Frowning, he carried the sack of food over to the platform where Melvin was attaching wires to the large lower jaw of the dragon.

Stone's sharp gaze caught a glimpse of the other man's red-rimmed eyes as he accepted the sack Stone had handed him. Melvin's mumbled thank you was nearly lost in the rustling of the paper he unfolded from a thick sandwich.

More to get information than to make polite conversation, Stone asked, "How's it going?"

"Another couple of days should do it," Melvin said around a mouthful of sandwich.

"Twenty-four-hour days?"

Melvin's reply was a garbled mumble that could have been either a yes or a no. The sandwich was more important to Whitney's partner than conversation.

His gaze on Whitney sleeping in the chair, Stone half sat on the edge of the platform. Crossing his arms over his chest, he asked a question he wasn't sure he wanted answered. "What's next after the dragon?"

"Don't ask. We've got more orders than we can handle. All we need is four more hands and forty-eight-hour days."

Stone spun his head around to look at Melvin. The proverbial light bulb flashed as an idea sprang into his head. It was such an easy solution, it was amazing no one had thought of it before.

Melvin scowled in puzzlement when he saw Stone's expression. "We used an expression just like yours on the Cheshire cat for the Alice in Wonderland display. What's up, Prince?"

By now Stone was used to the nickname and ignored it. He had other more important things to discuss with Melvin and he had to do it while Whitney was asleep. He glanced again at her, then brought his attention back to Melvin. "While you're finishing your sandwich, I have something I want to discuss with you."

Ten

The dragon was magnificent when it was finished. The shiny scarlet-and-gold material sewn by three women fit perfectly, effectively hiding the metal framework and all the wiring it took to make the dragon's mouth open and close and his body to undulate. It was one of the largest designs Grant and Gun had ever made and one of the most glorious.

On Friday a rented flatbed truck delivered the dragon to the Chinese Culture Center in Chinatown, and Melvin and Whitney went to test it after it was set up. No matter how many times the mechanical figures were checked and rechecked at the warehouse, transporting them occasionally caused problems. Whitney had her fingers crossed this wasn't one of those times, and held her breath when Melvin flipped the switch.

She stood with the officials from the culture center and watched as the dragon's head began moving. Its mouth opened, and brilliant colored silk "flames" rippled and waved as though the dragon were breathing

fire. It worked perfectly. Amid applause and congratu-
lations, Whitney joined Melvin and helped gather up
the tools they had brought with them just in case.

After every design was completed, especially one as
complicated as the dragon, there was always a feeling
of anticlimax. Despite all the hard work and all the
problems, the challenge had been fun, and now it was
over. There was always another project waiting to be
worked on, more difficulties to be overcome, but she
always experienced a let-down feeling after completing
a complicated design. Maybe that was part of the satisfaction she got out of doing what she did.

Back at the warehouse, she plopped down in her
chair and put her feet up on her desk. She had returned to the warehouse to be there when Stone arrived as he had every night after he left work. Glancing
at her watch, she saw that it was seven o'clock, well
past the time Stone usually came with their dinner.
Maybe she should go home and catch up on her sleep.
Except she didn't have the energy at the moment to get
out of the chair.

Melvin pulled out his chair and collapsed into it. "I'm
going to go home and sleep for the next week," he said
wearily.

"That's fine, as long as your week ends on Monday,"
she murmured, resting her head on the back of the
chair. "The Rose Bowl Parade mockup has to be finished by the end of the month, remember?"

"Along with three other projects. Plus the ones scheduled to be taken down." His chair squeaked as he
swirled it around so he was facing her. "I do believe the
time has come for us to think about getting some
help."

She jerked her head down to stare at him. "Help? What kind of help?"

"Like a few more hands and brains."

"What are you talking about, Melvin? I'm too tired for games."

"Well, you and I have created our own little monster, Whitney. We have gotten so successful, we can't handle it all by ourselves."

"We've been handling things just fine."

"Yeah, sure," her partner scoffed. "By nearly killing ourselves. The other night Prince made a suggestion I've been mulling over, and I've come to the conclusion he was right."

Whitney brought her feet down to the floor and leaned her forearms on the top of her desk. "What suggestion did Stone make?"

"That we hire extra hands and brains, a couple of computer technicians or electrical wizards with an interest in animated figures. I don't know why we didn't think of it ourselves. If we had a few more people working for us, we wouldn't have to kill ourselves meeting deadlines."

Whitney didn't know what surprised her more, the idea of hiring extra personnel or the fact that Stone was the one who suggested it. She frowned as she wondered why he had mentioned it to Melvin and not to her. Of course, there hadn't been much opportunity to talk this past week, although apparently Stone had managed to discuss his idea with her partner.

"Well, do I start looking for new recruits?" Melvin asked.

She rested her chin in her hand to support her weary head. "I haven't had time to think about it, for Pete's sake. There're a number of things to consider before we hire someone to work with us. Like whether we can afford it."

"We can. Prince has done something called a feasibility study. We can double our income and output if we hire two technicians. If we hired more than two, we would need bigger premises, but the extra expense would be compensated for by the additional income."

Whitney stared at her partner. "It sounds like we haven't been the only ones busy this week."

Melvin grinned. "I think it has something to do with his wanting you to have more free time. Heaven knows what he wants you to do with all this extra time he's trying to find for you."

"He doesn't seem to be all that eager. I don't see him anywhere around, do you?"

"Now that you mention it, I do notice that our supply sergeant hasn't arrived with our dinner. It looks like we're going to have to fend for ourselves." He stood up. "I for one am going home to become better acquainted with my bed. I suggest you do the same."

Whitney remained in her chair after Melvin was gone. She tried to remember what Stone had said before he left last night, but the day was a complete blur. She couldn't recall a single thing he had said about today other than asking if the dragon was going to be done on time. He had kissed her briefly and disappeared sometime in the early evening.

So where was he now? she asked herself silently.

When Stone did turn up, Whitney was sound asleep in the chair. For a long moment, he stared down at her. Her dark lashes lay against her soft cheeks and there were purple shadows of exhaustion under her eyes. A muscle clenched in his jaw. He hated this. He really hated seeing her wear herself out, getting only enough sleep to barely keep her going. She might think she could work like that forever, but he wasn't so sure he could continue watching her drive herself into the ground during these intense work sessions.

She didn't wake when he lifted her into his arms. Her head lolled onto his shoulder and she mumbled under her breath as he carried her out to his car. Something was going to have to be done about her backbreaking work schedule. He wanted a full-time relationship with her, not a few moments stolen in between animated dragons and monkeys.

A little later when he started to remove her clothes after placing her on her bed, she slowly opened her eyes and murmured, "Hi."

"Hi."

"The dragon's all done," she slurred sleepily as he slid her arm out of a sleeve.

"So are you," he said dryly. "At least for tonight."

"It was really beautiful. You should have seen it."

He scowled. "I've seen it." He was heartily sick of the blasted dragon. He would be perfectly happy if he never had to see it again.

It was a minor struggle to get a nightgown on her because she was limp with exhaustion and not entirely helpful. He held her up in a sitting position as he tried to get one of her arms into a sleeve, but she wanted to slide her arm around his neck to bring him closer.

He caught her wrist and gently guided her arm into the sleeve. His attention had been on the job at hand, but when he brought his gaze back to her face, he saw her pouting lips. Smiling, he let his finger trail over her bottom lip. "What's this for?"

"I've missed you," she said simply.

Desire flared within him, but he tamped it down. "I haven't gone anywhere."

"You haven't touched me in years."

It seemed that long to him, too, but this wasn't the time to do anything about it. She was completely exhausted and needed sleep, not lovemaking.

He covered her with the sheet and blankets and remained beside her on the bed, although it was difficult to resist the temptation to lie down and take her into his arms.

He leaned over to kiss her lightly. "You don't plan on going to the warehouse tomorrow, do you?"

She shook her head. "Monday."

"Did Melvin mention anything about hiring more help?"

"Hmmm."

Unsatisfied with her answer, he prodded. "Well? What did you think of the idea?"

Her hand raised limply, then fell again. Her eyes closed as she mumbled, "It takes time."

She was half asleep but he persisted, "What takes time?"

"Finding the right people." She sighed heavily. "Why isn't there ever enough time?" Without waiting for an answer, she rolled onto her side and fell into a deep sleep.

Stone let his fingers brush over her hair as he thought about what she had said. Then he tucked the blankets over her shoulders and stood up.

Remaining beside her bed, he stared down at her for several minutes. When he at last came to a decision he left her bedroom, quietly shutting the door behind him.

• • •

Whitney slept for nearly twelve hours. When she opened her eyes she tried to remember how she had gotten home, but had only a vague recollection of Stone putting her to bed.

Flinging her arms over her head, she stretched luxuriously on the cool sheets, a smile curving her lips. The whole day, the whole weekend was spread out in front of her. She would be able to be with Stone now without the interference of her work.

She glanced at the blue sky outside her window. It looked like a perfect day for a picnic. As soon as Stone called or came over, she was going to suggest they go to Golden Gate Park again, unless he had made other plans for their weekend. She felt as though a heavy weight had been lifted from her shoulders, and bounded out of bed to get ready.

At noon, Stone still hadn't phoned or arrived at her apartment. When she called his home, there was no answer. Ringing his office even though it was Saturday, she came up with the same result.

During the rest of the day and all day Sunday, Whitney was alone in her apartment, alternately pacing the floor, staring out the window of her living room, and calling Stone's home. By Sunday evening she didn't know whether to be worried or angry. He had wanted her to spend time with him and now that she was free, he was nowhere around.

By late Sunday night, she had gone past coming up with excuses why he hadn't contacted her. She no longer thought he might have been in an accident, had amnesia, or contracted the bubonic plague. He had apparently been all right when he had brought her home from the warehouse.

Lying in her bed that night, she began to wonder if

Stone was staying away from her on purpose, wanting her to think about the way their relationship was going . . . or wasn't going. There had to be a reason why he had been so attentive all week when she couldn't spare him much time, and why he was virtually ignoring her now that she was free.

On Monday she was no closer to coming up with the reason Stone had disappeared from her life. Before she joined Melvin at the drawing board, she phoned Stone's office and was told by his secretary that he was out of town. Putting down the phone, Whitney was at a complete loss. Unfamiliar insecurity gnawed at her. Strange questions came from nowhere to whirl around inside her mind. Was he really out of town, or had he instructed his secretary to tell her that? If he was going out of town, why hadn't he told her? When would he be back? Where in hell was he?

Around one o'clock, Whitney went to Nancy's shop to take down the teddy tree. Several hours later she returned to the warehouse with the bears. She had to remove the wiring boards from the bears and then return them to Nancy. As she approached the door of the warehouse with an armful of the stuffed animals, the unexpected sound of voices greeted her. She peered over the top of the teddy bear's head to see what the commotion could possibly be.

She stopped suddenly at the sight of over a dozen people standing in front of the door, and one of the teddy bears toppled off the heap in her arms. A young man near her bent down to pick it up. Since her hands were occupied and he didn't know what to do with the rescued bear, he asked, "Would you like me to carry this one in for you?"

"Thanks," she said distractedly. She looked around

at the crowd of men and women. Some were dressed in suits, some in casual clothes, and all carried portfolios or attaché cases. She guessed their ages to be in the early twenties. They were all looking at her with mixed expressions.

She turned to the young man who was holding the bear. "What's going on? Why are you all here?"

"We're applying for the job."

"What job?"

"The one Professor Strainer told us about. Do you work here?"

"Yes. Who's Professor Strainer?"

"He's our professor at UC," a young woman with strawberry blond hair answered. She reached for the bear dangling precariously from Whitney's hand by one paw and examined the wires attached to its back. "Is this one of Grant and Gunn's creations?"

Whitney nodded. The woman had said UC, which meant they were all from the University of California at Berkeley. She watched as a number of the others came forward to examine the bear. From their comments, she could tell they were all acknowledgable about electrical wiring boards, and their curiosity and enthusiasm were obvious in their expressions.

The door slid open and Melvin appeared with a bearded young man at his side. When he caught sight of the crowd, his eyes widened in surprise. Then he saw Whitney and sighed with relief. "It's about time you got here."

She edged her way through the students to Melvin. "Do you know what this is all about?"

He nodded, looking slightly harassed. "Prince has sent us some applicants to interview."

Before Whitney had a chance to reply to that astounding

pronouncement, Melvin asked, "How do you want to handle this? I was going to take them one at a time, but that was when there were only a few. How about giving them all a tour and explaining what we do, and whoever is still interested afterwards can fill out an application?"

Whitney was still working on Stone's having sent all these students to the warehouse. Melvin's suggestion was as good as anything she could come up with at the moment, so she nodded. "Let me get rid of these bears first."

Much of the rest of the afternoon was spent in giving the students a tour. It took up a considerable amount of time, for each animated figure they had in stock was thoroughly examined and exclaimed over. They checked the students' qualifications, and they were extensive. Each one was taking a summer course from the professor they had mentioned and all had been highly recommended. The students filled out the applications Melvin had bought at a nearby office supply store, then they were finally sent on their way. Melvin and Whitney promised to let them know as soon as possible whether they were hired.

The following day there were several more applicants. This time they were professional designers from Silicon Valley, all extremely qualified and interested in the concept Melvin and Whitney had created. There were also two phone calls from Los Angeles that afternoon, one from a man and the other from a woman. Both asked to have job applications sent to them.

By evening Whitney felt as though they were under a state of siege. Melvin had said he thought Stone was behind this sudden influx of designers interested in working for Grant and Gunn, and she had a feeling he was right. She didn't have any problem with the idea of hiring additional personnel, yet she did object to Stone taking it upon himself to send people to them without discussing it first.

It was time to show Mr. Efficiency that he still had a lot to learn about relationships, at least this one with her.

A phone call to his office met with the same result as the previous day. Mr. Hamilton was out of town.

Well, he had to come home sometime.

Hours later, Whitney parked the van in Stone's driveway and opened the wide doors in back. She should have asked Melvin to help her lug the figure she had brought with her, but she didn't want him to know what she was going to do with it. She had wondered how she was going to sneak out the five-foot-tall figure without Melvin seeing her, but luckily he had had his fill of phone calls and applications and had left the warehouse before her.

Since the figure was heavy and cumbersome, Whitney got out a hand cart just before pulling the figure out of the van. Using the housekey Stone had given her, she unlocked the door and maneuvered the dolly into the house. A half hour later she came back out with the empty dolly.

Stone's flight arrived a little after ten that night and he drove directly home. He was tired, but it had been worth all the hours in the air and knocking on doors if some of the people he had contacted came through.

He dropped his overnight case on the floor in the hall without turning on the light. As he walked toward his bedroom, he removed his jacket, loosened his tie, and unbuttoned his collar. He debated calling Whitney, but it was late and he hoped she had sense enough to be in bed asleep. If not, he didn't want to know if she was still at the warehouse.

He wondered again, for about the hundredth time, whether he should have told Whitney what he was doing. She was probably concerned that he hadn't been to the warehouse or called her in the last few days. Perhaps it would have been wise, he conceded, to at least tell her what he was going to do since it was her business, but his patience and his sense of fair play had both been used up during the last week. He knew he couldn't blame her if she wasn't particularly happy about his interfering with the running of her company. He rubbed the back of his neck to ease the tense muscle there. There was still time. He would tell her tomorrow before the applicants started contacting Grant and Gunn.

He walked into his bedroom, flicked on the light switch, and froze.

He was wrong. He didn't have time to tell Whitney what he had been doing. She already knew. Standing beside his bed was a man dressed in white pants, a black-and-white striped shirt, and a black cap. A football referee. As soon as the light switch went on, there had been a whirring noise and now he could see what caused it. The referee's hands were moving. The palm of one hand came down to touch the outstretched fingers of the other hand in a gesture football fans everywhere recognized as a signal for time out.

Circling the figure, he ran his gaze from top to bottom searching for a note from Whitney, but didn't find one. He stopped in front and watched the hands move together and then apart. There was a message after all.

It took him a couple of seconds to find the switch to deactivate the referee, then he moved it to one side of the room. With a small smile curving his lips, he patted Whitney's mechanical emissary on its padded rear end. The message was received.

Whitney had been a little too generous with her favorite bubble bath. As she stepped into the bathtub, the scented bubbles completely covered the surface of the water, filling the bathroom with their jasmine fragrance. Leaning her head back, she closed her eyes and let the perfumed warmth seep into her. She had no idea what time it was and at the moment she really didn't care. The steamy air and heated water eased the tension she had been under for the last four days, and she gave in to the hedonistic pleasure of her bath.

When a cool draft suddenly changed the temperature of the room, she opened her eyes and saw Stone leaning casually against the doorway.

He was dressed in snug jeans and a white cotton pullover, the long sleeves pushed up on his forearms. Amusement and something else in his eyes made them seem brighter than she remembered. Her heart thudded painfully as she gazed hungrily at him.

"Enjoying the view?" she asked.

"Very much."

She shivered as much from his blatantly sensual expression as the coolness from the open door, and sank lower into the water. "You're letting in a draft."

"Sorry," he drawled, not sounding at all apologetic.

He stepped into the room, and his eyes never left hers as he closed the door. Two long strides brought him to the tub. He knelt beside it, his eyes level with hers, his arms resting on the rim of the tub. Even though the bubbles effectively hid most of her naked body from his view, she felt exposed and vulnerable with him so close.

"How long do these bubbles usually last?" he asked curiously.

"I've never timed them."

His fingers glided onto her shoulder and down her arm until they reached the surface of the water. Then they retraced the path up her shoulder and slowly edged down the gentle slope of her breast.

She tried to evade his tantalizing fingers, but the narrow tub didn't give her much room to navigate. "Don't change the subject," she muttered.

His hand stilled and he blinked in complete bewilderment. "What subject? We weren't talking."

"I'm still mad at you."

He withdrew his hand, resting his arm again on the edge of the tub. His expression was mildly curious and without a shred of guilt. "Why?"

It was extremely difficult to maintain a degree of indignation under her present naked circumstances, but she gave it a try. "You know why. You've been out recruiting half of California as job applicants for Grant and Gunn. Who put you in charge of procuring employees?"

"You did."

She gaped at him. "When did I do that?" she asked cautiously.

"Friday night when I brought you home from the warehouse. I asked you what you thought about hiring extra help, and you said you didn't have the time to find qualified people. So I found them for you."

Her deep sigh rippled the water slightly, and Stone shifted his gaze to the bubbles gliding gently over her skin. A shaft of desire hardened his body and had him gripping the enameled edge of the tub. It was difficult to concentrate on anything but the need to slide his hands over her skin.

When she spoke, he returned his gaze to hers. "I don't remember," she admitted sheepishly.

He frowned. "You don't remember my undressing you and putting you to bed?"

She shook her head.

He was definitely not pleased with her answer. "Whitney, are you telling me just any man could undress you and tuck you into bed and you wouldn't notice who in hell it was?"

Something in his outraged protest made her smile. "I knew it was you. I just don't remember anything we said." She lifted a soapy hand out of the water to cover his. "If we were in a dark room with a hundred people, I would know it was you the instant you touched me. No one else touches me the way you do, and I don't mean just physically."

His voice became husky with deep emotion. "Whitney, last week was pure hell. I was actually jealous of that damn dragon because he was taking you away from me. Something had to be done about your marathon work schedule and I couldn't wait until you eventually found the time to advertise for qualified help. I contacted an old college buddy who teaches at UC, and he promised to spread the word to some of his students about the job opportunity. From there I went to San Jose and Santa Clara where I had some business contacts who worked in Silicon Valley. Then I flew to Los Angeles to meet with several associates of Paul Strainer, who's a professor at UC. My flight got in about an hour ago."

"Why didn't you call me?"

"It was late when I got home. I thought you would be

in bed. Then I saw the large message you left in my room and decided to come over whether you were in bed or not." His sudden smile was soft and sensual. "I was disappointed when I went into your bedroom and you weren't there, but then I opened this door and found you covered in bubbles."

"I didn't mean tonight," she said. The hurt and disappointment of the last four days were apparent in her voice. "Why didn't you let me know what you were doing? I didn't know what to think when I didn't see you over the weekend, and then when I called your office on Monday, your secretary told me you were out of town. I didn't know what to think."

He saw the pain in her eyes and needed to erase it. Swiftly he plunged his hands into the water and lifted her out of the tub, bubbles and all. When her feet touched the tiled floor, he pulled her into his arms and lowered his head.

The moment his lips covered hers, the kiss was deep and hungry and intimate. Her skin was slick as his hands roamed over her back, and the fragrance of her flesh clouded his senses.

Tearing his mouth from hers, he buried his face in her hair. "Oh, God, Whitney. I missed you like hell. I felt as though my skin was being peeled away from my body when I reached out for you in lonely hotel rooms and you weren't there. I need you so much. With all the flying and meetings, though, the only times I could call you were in the middle of the night. Besides, I wanted to tell you in person what I was doing."

She wound her arms around his neck and held on tightly. "When you didn't call or didn't come, I thought you were ending it between us."

He jerked his head up so he could see her face. Her

hands dropped to his shoulders. "How could you think that? I love you."

All her doubts disappeared as she saw his words reflected in his eyes. "I love you too. Before I met you, I thought Grant and Gunn was enough to give me satisfaction and contentment, but now I know the whole business could disappear and my life would go on. But I don't want to live my life without you in it."

His smile was tender and full of love. "Then we'd better call Sylvia."

"Sylvia? Why?"

"To plan our wedding."

His marriage proposal took her completely by surprise. "But you said you didn't plan on getting married."

"I didn't plan on falling in love either. Marry me, Whitney. I want our relationship to be permanent with all the ties possible. I want to have children's fingerprints on the furniture and peanut-butter-and-jelly sandwiches for picnics at the beach and sand from little feet scattered all over the floor of my car."

Whitney's head spun. Marriage, children, and Stone. It was more than she had hoped, more than she had ever dreamed she would have. She saw uncertainty enter his eyes when she didn't answer immediately, and flung her arms around his neck.

"We don't need Sylvia. We don't need tuxedoes and tight shoes in order to get married."

"I don't care how we do it as long as it's soon. I find I have a possessive streak where you're concerned."

Her skin was cool under his hands and he reached for a towel off the nearest rack. Draping it around her shoulders, he said softly, "Why didn't you tell me you were getting cold?"

"I didn't notice," she replied honestly. Seeing how

damp his front had become, she added, "I'm getting your clothes all wet."

His smile was full of male promise. "I don't plan on having them on much longer."

"Are you planning on going home to bed soon?" she asked silkily, pressing her hips against his.

He picked her up, towel and all, and carefully maneuvered through the doorway and into her bedroom. "I am home," he said, setting her down on her bed. "Wherever you are is home."

She looked up at him and smiled. "Welcome home."

THE EDITOR'S CORNER

We have some deliciously heartwarming and richly emotional LOVESWEPTs for you on our holiday menu next month.

Judy Gill plays Santa by giving us **HENNESSEY'S HEAVEN,** LOVESWEPT #294. Heroine Venny Mc-Clure and a tantalizing hunk named Hennessey have such a sizzling attraction for each other that mistletoe wouldn't be able to do its job around them . . . it would just shrivel under their combined heat. Venny has come to her family-owned island to retreat from the world, not to be captivated by the gloriously hand-some and marvelously talented Hennessey. And he knows better than to rush this sweet-faced, sad-eyed woman, but her hungry looks make him too impetuous to hold back. When the world intrudes on their hide-away and the notoriety in her past causes grief, Venny determines to free Hennessey . . . only to discover she has wildly underestimated the power of the love this irresistible man has for her.

Two big presents of love are contained in one pretty package in **LATE NIGHT, RENDEZVOUS,** LOVE-SWEPT #295, by Margaret Malkind. You get not only the utterly delightful love story of Mia Taylor and Boyd Baxter but also that of their wonderfully liberated parents. When Boyd first confronts Mia at the library where she works, he almost forgets that his purpose is to enlist her help in getting her mother to cool his father's affections and late-blooming romanticism. She's scarcely able to believe his tales of her "wayward" mother . . . much less the effect he has on her. Soon, teaming up to restrain the older folks, they're taking lessons in love and laughter from them!

Michael Siran is the star twinkling on the top of the brilliantly spangled **CAPTAIN'S PARADISE,** LOVESWEPT #296, by Kay Hooper. Now that tough,

(continued)

fearless man of the sea gets his own true love to last a lifetime. When Robin Stuart is rescued by Michael from the ocean on a dark and dangerous night, she has no way of knowing that it isn't mere coincidence or great good luck that brought him to her aid. Indeed, they are both deeply and desperately involved with bringing the same ruthless man to justice. Before love can blossom for this winning couple, both must face their own demons and find the courage to love. Join Raven Long and friends for another spellbinding romantic adventure as "Hagan Strikes Again!"

You'll feel as though your stocking were stuffed with bonbons when you read **SWEET MISERY**, LOVESWEPT #297, by Charlotte Hughes. Roxie Norris was a minister's daughter—but certainly no saint! —and she was determined to win her independence from her family. Tyler Sheridan, a self-made man as successful as he was gorgeous, owed her father a big favor and promised to keep an eye on her all summer long. But Tyler hadn't counted on Roxie being a sexy, smart spitfire of a redhead who would turn him on his ear. She is forbidden fruit, yet Tyler yearns to teach her the pleasures of love. How can he fight his feelings for Roxie when she so obviously is recklessly, wildly attracted to him? The answer to that question is one sizzling love story!

You'll love to dig into **AT FIRST SIGHT**, LOVESWEPT #298, by Linda Cajio. Angelica Windsor was all fire and ice, a woman who had intrigued and annoyed Dan Roberts since the day they'd met. Conflict was their companion at every meeting, it seemed, especially during one tough business negotiation. When they take a break and find a baby abandoned in Dan's suite, these two sophisticates suddenly have to pull together to protect the helpless infant. Angelica finds that her inhibitions dissolve as her maternal qualities grow . . . and Dan is as enchanted with her as he is

(continued)

filled with anxious yearning to make the delightful new family arrangement last forever. A piece of holiday cake if there ever was one!

There's magic in this gift of love from Kathleen Creighton, **THE SORCERER'S KEEPER,** LOVESWEPT #299. Never has Kathleen written about two more winsome people than brilliant physicist Culley Ward and charming homemaker Elizabeth Resnick. When Culley finds Elizabeth and her angelic little daughter on his doorstep one moonlit night, he thinks he must be dreaming . . . but soon enough the delightful intruders have him wide awake! Elizabeth, hired by Culley's mother to look after him while she's on a cruise, turns out to be everything his heart desires; Culley soon is filling all the empty spaces in Elizabeth's heart. But healing the hurts in their pasts takes a bit of magic and a lot of passionate loving, as you'll discover in reading this wonderfully heartwarming and exciting romance.

It gives me a great deal of pleasure to wish you, for the sixth straight year, a holiday season filled with all the best things in life—peace, prosperity, and the love of family and friends.

Sincerely,

Carolyn Nichols

Carolyn Nichols
Editor
LOVESWEPT
Bantam Books
666 Fifth Avenue
New York, NY 10103

NEW!

Handsome Book Covers Specially Designed To Fit Loveswept Books

Our new French Calf Vinyl book covers come in a set of three great colors— royal blue, scarlet red and kachina green.

Each 7" × 9½" book cover has two deep vertical pockets, a handy sewn-in bookmark, and is soil and scratch resistant.

To order your set, use the form below.